To Lou:—
Best Wishes!

Walt Wood

Nov. 2009

BILLY'S HEROES

By WALT WOOD

Illustrated by P. Nancarrow

Copyright © 2009 by Walt Wood

ISBN 0-7414-5489-0

Published by:

INFINITY
PUBLISHING.COM

1094 New DeHaven Street, Suite 100
West Conshohocken, PA 19428-2713
Info@buybooksontheweb.com
www.buybooksontheweb.com
Toll-free (877) BUY BOOK
Local Phone (610) 941-9999
Fax (610) 941-9959

Printed in the United States of America

Published July 2009

Introduction

Hypnotism in the 1850's was a relatively new "science" and some doctors expected it might bring great benefits to the practice of medicine. Dr. Antonio Dulcamara arrived in Sacramento in 1856 with a strong desire to study this further.

He soon found two patients who were willing to help with his experiments. Billy Costello, and his wife, Thalia, were eager participants in helping the doctor.

Just prior to each experiment they filled their minds with details of a particular historical figure (William Tell, Julius Caesar, George Washington, Cleopatra, and more). When they were under the hypnotic spell, they found themselves closely connected with an important event in that ancient person's life.

You, too, can experience those events along with Billy and Thalia, knowing that even though this is a fictional account, most of the details of those happenings, as related here, are accurate.

Contents

Chapter 1

Billy Meets Dr. Dulcamara

"Hello, sir, you must be Mr. Billy Costello," said the tall, well-dressed, bearded man as he reached out to shake Billy's hand.

"Yes, sir, I am he," smiled Billy, as he shook hands with the man. "*A votre service!*"

"Oh! You speak French?" exclaimed the tall man.

"No, not really," laughed Billy. "My wife has been teaching me some phrases and that one just slipped out, without my thinking of it."

"Well, it sounded very genuine," said the man. "I do speak French and it sounded quite right; your accent and pronunciation are quite correct."

"Let me introduce myself," he continued. "I'm Doctor Dulcamara, Antonio Dulcamara. I'm new in town and I was told to contact you. I hope to set up my practice here. I will need an advocate, a solicitor, a lawyer, as you call it. You have been highly recommended to me."

"Well, thank you sir," replied Billy. "I'm always pleased when someone speaks well of me. I am honest and I try to do my best. If that's what you're looking for in a lawyer, then perhaps we can form a team."

"You Americans have such a quaint way of putting things," laughed Dr. Dulcamara. "*Form a team* sounds so right, so correct. I like what you do with the language."

"Well, we're pretty much direct in what we say," answered Billy. "Not all of us, of course, but many of us do have the habit of trying to get to the point, to the heart of the

1

matter, and often that leads to expressions that sometimes hit the nail on the head."

"Ha! There's another," exclaimed Dr. Dulcamara. *"Hit the nail on the head*—it is so apt, it fits so well. I need to learn more of your phrases and I hope you will help me in that, in the future."

"Yes, yes, of course," replied Billy. "But, let us sit down and rest our legs. We can then be more comfortable as we talk."

They each took a chair, Billy in his desk-chair and Dr. Dulcamara in the chair next to Billy's desk.

Billy was a partner with Bert Jensen in their law office in Sacramento, California. Billy's wife, Thalia, was a highly-accomplished lady who spoke several languages and knew everything about everything, or so it seemed to her husband of three years. Billy was continually impressed with Thalia's knowledge and her easy manner of imparting that information to one and all, especially to Billy.

"I take it that you've recently arrived in the USA," said Billy, as he closely observed this newcomer to town.

"Yes," answered Dr. Dulcamara, "I landed in New York and was there for about two weeks, then I arranged transport to Independence, Missouri, then came by stage coach to here. I arrived four days ago. When I was in Europe, doing my medical studies, I always dreamed of going to California, a land that seemed magical to me."

"Upon my arrival in your city, I arranged for lodging," he went on, "and then began looking for a place to set up my medical practice. I went to your fine library to check out some maps and other information. It was there that I learned about you; the librarian highly praises your knowledge and ability."

"However, you do look very young to me," Dr. Dulcamara added, with gentleness and a smile. "I'm used to

2

older men, generally fifty and so years old, who are lawyers, like they are in Austria where I studied. I mean you no disrespect when I say that you seem to be very young."

"I am young," laughed Billy. "I'm twenty-four. But I've been counseling people for the last eight years, for a short while when I lived in Missouri and during the six years that I've lived here in California. Here, in the West, you'll find many very young people in responsible positions; they are presidents, vice-presidents, and other high officials even though they are less than thirty-five years old. Some are owners of shops and businesses. Some young people own ships and stage-coach lines; many are managers of banks."

"California is a very, very young country," he added. "One reason is because the trip across country is difficult for older people. So many of us who are new to California are in our early years. Many of us are quite young."

"I like that, you have youthful vigor," said Dr. Dulcamara, with a wide smile and with some admiration. "In Europe, where I've spent most of my life, a young person has some difficulty establishing himself. It was true in my case. The older physicians are set in their ways and are very resistant to new medical discoveries. But, we young doctors quickly grasp onto the new ideas, new ways to treat illnesses, new medicines and techniques. We are anxious to try new things, whereas the older medical people are careful and usually do things as they did them for years before; they don't change their ways or methods readily."

"My special field, my main interest," he added, taking on a more serious aspect, "is *hypnotism*. That's the common name for it but there are several other medical terms applied in medical practice. However, I'm happy with the name *hypnotism*. The name readily describes the technique and is a short word and easy to say by anyone. As you know, many medical terms are very long and hard to pronounce by the general public."

3

"Yes," laughed Billy, "some of them are a mouthful. I don't know how you doctors can handle them."

"Well," answered Dr. Dulcamara, "all of us, as medical students, had to learn Latin and Greek, and those two languages are the basis for nearly one-hundred percent of the medical terms. So, once you know those languages, you can more easily relate to the medical terms."

"But," said Billy, inquisitively, "tell me about hypnotism. I know nothing about it."

"Well, in a sense, it's mind over matter," replied Dr. Dulcamara. "Your deep-seated brain controls your body in ways that you may never have experienced before."

"A person, a patient, can enter a temporary state of semi-consciousness," he continued, "and while in that state, they can endure pain without feeling the pain. They can dream, as if they're asleep in their bed, a dream that seems to them to take days and days but in reality lasts only a few minutes. The patient can perform certain functions, such as making a speech, or going through various repetitive motions and exercises, easily and effectively."

"My Oh My!" exclaimed Billy. "That does sound interesting. I can see where a young doctor, like yourself, would be highly interested in that new method of treating illnesses. Is that your strong point? Did I understand you correctly?"

"Yes, yes," replied Dr. Dulcamara, enthusiastically and warming to his subject. "I'm one of the New Romans, sometimes called the New Greeks, meaning that we have taken up a new idea and begun to explore it. A few of us have embraced hypnotism in order to help people medically. I think that it has great promise."

"I intend to do some experiments," he continued, "and I'll need some one to help me. Perhaps you'll be interested in cooperating with me on this research?"

"Oh, yes," said Billy, eagerly. "From your description, I feel sure that I'd like to be part of your experiments. Of course, I'm not medically knowledgeable, I know little about medicine, but I'm willing to help. Please consider me wherever I can fit. I can be available most of the time, unless I'm tied up with a client or with a project."

"Fine," said the doctor, "I will be happy for you to participate with me in this new way to reach out to patients. But, I'm taking up too much of your time," he said apologetically. "Let us arrange a meeting where we can explore these ideas more fully."

"I'd certainly like to do that," said Billy, emphatically. "To me, this seems like a whole new approach to medicine, the idea of helping people in an unusual way. I'm very much interested in what you intend to do."

"And, of course, besides the experiments, I'd be happy to be your legal counsel, your lawyer," he added. "We can arrange the terms when we next meet. My wife will be highly interested in you and in hypnotism. She has traveled and lived in Europe. Besides English, she speaks Greek, Italian, and French. She will be as interested as I am in this new medical approach."

"Fine," said Dr. Dulcamara. "You are the man I want as my legal counsel. You sound very wise, well beyond your years," he laughed a little, but with a feeling of confidence, "and I'll contact you as soon as I get my office space developed and my office opened to the public."

"Good," said Billy, as both men stood up. "If you need help in finding a place, maybe I can help—at least, I'm willing to help. Meanwhile, I hope we can meet sooner rather than later. When you find time, we should have lunch together."

"That is a fine idea, and it will happen very soon, I'm sure," replied Dr. Dulcamara, as he put on his hat and turned to go.

5

Just then, Billy's partner, Bert Jensen, came in the front door.

"Bert," said Billy, "let me introduce Dr. Dulcamara. He's a new physician in town and has asked that we represent him in any legal matter."

The two men shook hands.

"I'm pleased to meet you," said Bert, with his big smile.

"Likewise," answered Dr. Dulcamara, who began to laugh loudly. "There—I used one of your new phrases," he said. "I answered '*likewise*' as if I'd been using that word for years" he continued to laugh, "but I learned it only recently. See, I am becoming Americanized!"

All three laughed as Billy led Dr. Dulcamara to the door and bade him "Good Day".

That evening, at supper, Billy told his wife, Thalia, about Dr. Dulcamara and hypnotism. Thalia listened closely to what Billy told her.

"I dimly remember hearing something about that when I was in Paris," she said. "But I didn't pay any attention to such items. A healthy young girl like me feels indestructible and spends no time listening to medical problems and cures."

"But," she went on, "there is a very interesting aspect to this hypnotism. Let's suppose, just suppose, mind you, that Dr. Dulcamara could put you to sleep so you could dream that you were with some famous person, at some famous event that took place in history."

"Think about it," she added, "you could be part of the group with Julius Caesar when he was preparing to go to the Senate on the Ides of March in 44 BC. That was the day that he was assassinated. Your dream might last only a few minutes, according to Dr. Dulcamara, but the events in your dream might involve a day or more, really an indefinite time!"

"I've often heard," she went on, "that the actual time that any of us dream is only for a minute or two but the dream-time, as we recall it later, often seems to have lasted for a long time, perhaps a day or more."

"Just think," she smiled and looked at the ceiling to see a housefly. The fly landed on the table and she swatted at it. "You could be an aide to Julius Caesar, and be in on all of the action on the Ides of March. You could experience all of the details of what was taking place at that time, almost as if you were a 'fly-on-the-wall'. Just like this fly that I'm swatting at!"

"We often hear people say that they'd like to have been a fly-on-the-wall during some special event," she added, "and with this hypnotism thing, you, Billy, **could be that fly-on-the-wall!** Oh, Oh! That appeals to me, doesn't it to you?"

"Yes, yes!" exclaimed Billy, feeding on his wife's excitement, and getting more excited himself. "You've just given me the idea that opens up a whole new world! Here's what we'll do."

Billy outlined to Thalia a plan whereby he would immerse himself in some historical event, such as Julius Caesar's assassination centuries ago. She would help him and they'd use whatever books from the library that were available. He would cram all the information shortly before Dr. Dulcamara was ready to put him under a hypnotic spell.

As he was being hypnotized, his mind would be full of that special historical event. He would expect to "dream" about it when he was unconscious! He could be present at the time of the Ides of March in ancient Rome!

Yes, that was the ticket! He could turn himself into a "living witness" of the event. He might be one of the men going with Caesar to the Senate on the day that he was killed, on the day, long ago, when the assassination took place.

Oh, there was so much to be involved in! He could stand next to King John as he signed the Magna Carta, to Julius Caesar, to William Tell, to Betsy Ross—he would be **right there** when the historic event happened!

Thalia's fly-on-the-wall idea was terrific and he would follow through with it. It would be almost like a new kind of parlor entertainment—and very educational.

"Now, hon," Billy said, after they'd more fully discussed her idea, "let's make a list of historical events, really outstanding events that have proved to be important in history."

"I'll do that, I'll make a list," said Thalia, picking up on Billy's enthusiasm, "and we'll go over it and choose which event you want to be involved with. Then, before he puts you "under" you'll think of nothing but that event. After you come out of it, maybe you'll be able to tell us what happened while you were in Dreamland. Oh! I'm so excited about doing this, I can't hold still!"

"And me, too," said Billy, excitedly. "Now, we haven't started anything yet, but I'm sure that the first session will be a trial session just to get me to understand what is going on, to get acquainted with his procedure. Then, the second or third session, will be my "dreamland" adventure"—probably the death of Caesar."

"You'll need to be with me," he continued, as he gave his wife a warm squeeze, "you should be watching me when I'm "under" so you can observe anything that might be of interest. Whatever you see, you can discuss with me when I wake up. Of course, the doctor will be observing me, too, I'm sure. After all, it's his experiment."

"True, true," said Thalia, "he really wants you to participate in his experiment. It is our idea that you try to dream of some historic event while you are asleep."

"In effect," said Billy, "there are two experiments going on at the same time—the doctor's medical experiment and our personal experiment."

"Yes," laughed Thalia. "Here, this new doctor comes to town and wants you to be his attorney and also cooperate with him in some medical experiments and, suddenly we find ourselves planning to dream about some important events in history! What an interesting road we are going to travel."

"Yes," replied Billy, "two weeks ago I had no inkling that I'd be involved with being present at some great historical event, and now I'm trying to be part of it. It's a magical world that we live in, darling!"

A few days later, Billy and the doctor had a long lunch, where the doctor explained his experimental techniques to Billy. The methods were non-intrusive; they involved no pain, and were unique. They would be unlike any previous medical experience that Billy had ever experienced. He readily agreed to participate.

Meanwhile, every evening Billy and Thalia studied a list of about twenty famous events that they could be part of. Thalia did not want to be left out of the testing and there were several famous women that she wanted to be connected with.

A week later, Dr. Dulcamara sent a messenger boy to Billy's office, to advise him that his office was now open and Billy was welcome to come in at any time, and that they might try out a short session of hypnosis.

Billy had just finished writing up some papers on a legal matter and he told the boy to go back to Dr. Dulcamara and tell him that he, Billy, along with his wife, Thalia, would be there within thirty minutes. When he finished his legal work, he walked the short distance to his home, gathered Thalia, and they both walked to the doctor's office.

When Billy and Thalia arrived in the waiting room, Dr. Dulcamara heard them and immediately came out and welcomed them. "Come into my office," he said, "and I'll explain what I am doing."

Dr. Dulcamara, on several previous occasions, when he had been invited to Billy's home, explained more details about his experiments. He had discussed hypnotism and how it worked.

Now, today he wanted to refresh them on its benefits and drawbacks. During his visits to Billy's home he had tasted Thalia's delicious cooking. He highly prized the food and fellowship of those meetings. He was especially impressed with Thalia's foreign-language ability and her knowledge of some of the countries of Europe.

"Now, Billy," said Dr. Dulcamara. "This will be the first session and it will be very short. Some people cannot be hypnotized but if you will follow my directions, I'm quite sure that it will work for you."

"Mrs. Costello," he said to Thalia, "you may sit in this chair and be your own observer."

Dr. Dulcamara sat Billy in a comfortable, leather-covered, reclining couch. It had a hinged back and easily became a reclining sofa or a couch. He sat in a chair beside Billy. He asked Billy what he'd like to think about and Billy said "Julius Caesar".

"Ah! The long-ago leader of the Romans, who was killed in the Senate?" said Dr. Dulcamara.

"Yes," answered Billy. "He was one of the most famous Romans and every schoolboy knows about him."

"I would like for you to hold that dream about Caesar until the next session," said the doctor. "I'd much prefer if you, during this first session, were to think about some event in your own personal past."

"All right," replied Billy, "I'll try to recall some part of my trip West, when I came to California for the first time."

"Now, keep in mind," said the doctor, "the idea of yours to dream about some historical event is fine and I have no objection, but my real purpose is to evaluate your actions while you are 'under'. I may take this tiny pin and touch your skin with it to see if you later can tell me that you felt some small pain. Also, I may have you stand and exercise while you are 'under'. Anything that I will request that you do, will be gentle and you need not fear it or them. Your wife will be watching all of these actions and I will confer with her as I need to."

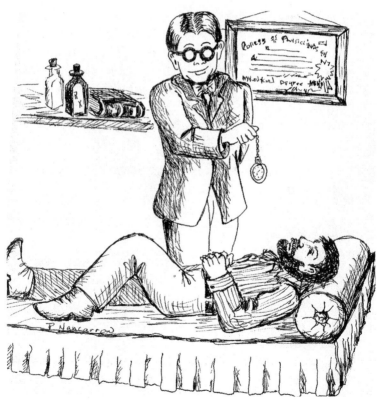

Billy is ready to enter Dreamland

Billy nodded his head in agreement. He was comfortable as he sat on the couch. Thalia sat in a chair nearby.

Dr. Dulcamara began to talk in a very low voice, quietly, gently, and warmly. Very soon Billy seemed to doze off. His hands fell to his sides. Dr. Dulcamara began to make notes. He wrote down the time; it was 2:28pm when Billy began his "sleep".

The doctor quietly observed Billy as he lay, appearing to be comfortably asleep. He took his blood pressure, counted his pulse, and his breathing rhythm and recorded the numbers on his tablet pad. At times, the doctor walked around to observe Billy from other angles.

Thalia watched everything and paid particular attention to what Billy was doing.

After a few minutes, the doctor took a tiny pin and, signaling to Thalia to watch, he jabbed the pin into Billy's finger. There was no reaction. Billy did not feel any pain. Again, he jabbed the pin in the back of Billy's hand. Again, there was no reaction—apparently no pain.

He gently told Billy to stand and when he did, he asked him to stand on one leg and twirl, keeping his balance. Billy performed the maneuver expertly.

"He could never do that at home," laughed Thalia. "He'd have fallen on his face!"

The doctor smiled. The experiment was going well and he was happy with the data he was collecting.

Occasionally, Billy smiled, other times he frowned. When he lay back on the couch, at times he raised his arms above his head and then out in front of him. Sometimes, he squirmed, as if he was in some kind of trouble. At several times, he appeared to be riding a horse.

At times his pulse raced and his blood pressure rose dramatically. The doctor made notes of all of these actions. Never once did Billy seem to be fearful of anything. He was happy with whatever adventure was happening in his unconscious mind.

After Dr. Dulcamara had gathered what he felt was sufficient information, he sat in the chair next to Billy and gently spoke his name and snapped his fingers. Billy awoke at once. He had been asleep for exactly eight minutes.

His eyes opened and he quickly looked around to see where he was. Immediately, he realized he was in Dr. Dulcamara's office and the good doctor was smiling at him. There was Thalia, sitting in the chair next to the doctor.

"Well, how was that?" asked Dr. Dulcamara, gently.

"Fine," answered Billy. "I feel as if I'd just taken a short nap, forty winks worth. But I'm fully awake now."

"Well," said the doctor, "you were asleep for exactly eight minutes."

"Eight minutes!" exclaimed Billy, as he shook his head in disbelief.

"Did you feel any pain?" asked the doctor.

"No, none whatsoever," answered Billy.

"Did you experience any exercise?"

"No, nothing," said Billy. "I'm pretty sure that all I did was lie here on the couch the whole time."

"Well," said the doctor, "I had you do some simple exercise, balancing on one foot. Also, I touched you lightly with a sharp pin, to see if you'd wince and you did not."

"No," replied Billy, "I didn't experience any balancing exercise, nor was I aware that you'd stuck me with a pin."

"Good, fine," said the doctor, happily confirming those reactions in his patient.

"Did you dream about anything?" the doctor asked.

13

"Oh, yes," said Billy, "I was saying goodbye to my aunt and uncle back in Missouri, as I was leaving them to go to California. I'd got on my horse and was waving to them, as I rode toward the wagon train. Then, it was several days later, and my horse stepped in a gopher hole and broke his leg. That meant that the horse had to be put to sleep, but I couldn't do it. My horse was my friend. He was like a good buddy to me. But there was no chance to save him, no chance that he could live, so I asked the wagon-train master to solve the problem."

"The wagon-train master said he'd take care of it. I chose another horse and rode far, far ahead so I wouldn't hear the shot and sure enough I heard nothing. I had gone ahead and found our campsite for the overnight rest stop and was getting the area ready when I woke up, and there were you and Thalia. My dream was just as real as if it had truly happened. Of course, it did actually happen to me but that was six years ago!"

The doctor had Billy stand up and walk about for a few moments, which he did easily. The doctor took more readings of blood pressure, respiration, and heart beat.

"That's fine, Billy," said Dr. Dulcamara. "No pain, a real life-like dream, and no dizziness or any ill effects after you woke up."

"Right," said Billy. "I'm impressed. How long did you say I was "out"?"

"Exactly eight minutes," said the doctor. "While you were sleeping, I monitored your pulse, your blood pressure, your breathing, and your general aspects. There was nothing out of line."

"Now, you said earlier," said Billy, "that a dentist could pull a diseased tooth and the patient would feel no pain during the operation?"

"That's right," replied Dr. Dulcamara. "That's what I want to establish in my experiments. The patient will probably have pain after they wake up due to the tooth being taken out, but they would have no pain during the actual extraction of the tooth—and that's what most people fear, the terrible pain associated with the act of pulling the tooth. They can more readily stand the pain **after** the extraction, it's the pain **during** the extraction that is tough for them to bear."

"Well, that makes sense," said Billy. "I'm impressed. I'm amazed. I really don't know what to say. You've demonstrated to me what a new and novel way that this hypnotism works. Let's do another session as soon as you can find the time."

"Honey, you were marvelous," said Thalia, as she gently squeezed his arm. "We guessed that you were dreaming because sometimes you'd laugh a little and once or twice you had a deep frown on your face. When we get home, you'll have to tell me more about your dream."

"Billy, you were a perfect patient!" exclaimed the doctor, very pleased with the results of this first test. "You've helped me in my experimenting. You are helping me expand the knowledge of using hypnotism for medical reasons and so I'm grateful to you."

"Well, it doesn't seem to hurt me any," said Billy. "So let's keep it going. We can schedule another session as soon as we both have time."

"Excellent," said Dr. Dulcamara, happily satisfied with the results of this first session with Billy. "The next time, I'll try to keep you sleeping for about ten or fifteen minutes, maybe a little longer."

"That's alright with me," said Billy. "I'm game and I trust you not to hurt me."

"Never fear," replied the doctor. "I will do nothing that will be harmful to you."

"Soon, doctor," said Thalia, "you'll have to consider me as one of your test-patients."

"Oh yes, my dear, certainly" he replied. "That's a good idea. You have already used your finely-tuned observational skills to help with this session and you'll be very helpful if you undergo my hypnosis. You and your husband are two very fine patients, and I'm happy that you are helping me in my endeavors. I feel very fortunate, indeed."

"Well, we both can see some promise in what you are doing," she said, "and we are happy to be on the cutting edge of your research. You are open and honest about your efforts and we both hope that your results will be beneficial to everyone."

"I'll say 'Amen' to that," said Billy, emphasizing what Thalia had just stated. "We want to help you."

"I am deeply grateful to both of you," smiled the doctor. "I am so lucky to have you as willing patients. I will not betray your trust in me."

Billy and Thalia said goodbye to the doctor and walked home, feeling that they'd both been involved in a grand experiment in the medical field.

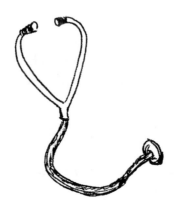

Chapter 2

King John and the Magna Carta

"Billy," said Dr. Dulcamara, "are you ready for the treatment? Has Thalia prepared you, gotten you ready for your great experiment?" He said the latter with a little laugh, partly to put Billy at ease.

"Oh, yes," replied Billy. "I'm so stuffed full of information that I'm ready to burst. My wife knows everything about everything. She is so smart and knowledgeable. She even had a special book on the Magna Carta."

"So, it's the Magna Carta that you're prepared to be part of, is it?" asked the doctor. "Let's see, didn't that take place in the early 1200's or so?"

"Yes, 1215 to be exact," replied Billy. "That's the date that Thalia gave me and I'll bet my life it's the exact date!"

"Well, you certainly do have full confidence in your wife," smiled the doctor.

"That's right," said Billy, almost laughing, "she's right! There's no two ways about it. For the past few days, she's been telling me of the troubles that the barons in early England were having with King John. They'd been given certain rights earlier, but King John kept whittling those rights away and the barons were not happy. They had complained but their complaints had fallen on deaf ears; the king would not respond favorably to their petitions."

"He spent a lot of money, their money," Billy continued, "on a war in France and now he wanted to tax them some more to make up the deficit. That's when they said: "Enough!"

"Several times, the barons sent some representatives to the king," he added, "but the king paid no attention to their pleas. Now they had formed a group to demand their rights. They put together a strong body, practically an army, to march on London and insist that King John make reforms."

"Well," said the doctor, "you do sound well prepared. So, let's get to it. As explained earlier, I want you to lie on the couch here. Be very comfortable; if you're not, make sure you tell me, so we can make adjustments beforehand."

"I will put you to sleep, under hypnosis," he added, "You will have no ill effects from this, but I am hoping that you will have a fine, lengthy experience, an experience that you can tell me about when you wake up. You will be asleep for about twenty or thirty minutes, but it may seem like a few days or a week or two to you while you are under."

"Sounds good to me," said Billy. "Oh, there's Thalia. Hello, honey," he said as his wife came into the room. "I'm about to go under, to be hypnotized, and I'm hoping that I'll dream about King John and the Magna Carta, using all of that historical information that you've been stuffing me with the past few days."

"I hope so, too," said Thalia, as she bussed Billy on the cheek, "it will make a grand story if it works out as we've planned."

"Doctor," she said as she turned to Dr. Dulcamara, "do you think he will dream about the Magna Carta?"

"Well, of course, that is what I'm trying to research and to make happen, if possible," replied the doctor. "If I can get Billy to sleep and then have him dream about a certain historical event, it will further my research immeasurably. Let's hope for the best."

"All right, Billy," said the doctor. "This is what I want you to do." He explained the short procedure as Billy lay on the couch. The doctor, turned serious, touched Billy on the forehead, then he gently laid his hand on his face and quick as a wink, Billy was in dreamland. Dr. Dulcamara and Thalia sat in chairs next to the couch and observed Billy.

As he entered his dream state, Billy seemed to be part of a group of barons. He was standing by a fireplace in a tavern. There were about fifteen or twenty people gathered around the fireplace.

"I tell you, sir," said Adam Hugh, "we've no right to tell the King what to do! He's the King, given to us by God and we must obey him, just as we should obey God!" Adam was a loyalist and was quick to condemn the barons for rising up against the king.

"Well," replied Alan Basset, "we are NOT slaves! The King is NOT Almighty! You can say that God appointed him, but that's not my belief, that's your belief. My belief is that God doesn't appoint anybody—that's just a story put out by rulers to convince people that God is backing them."

Adam Hugh shrunk back as Alan said those words. He seemed to be fearful that a thunderbolt might suddenly come racing from above to slam into Alan.

He looked about the room. The men, all Englishmen and all barons, earls, knights, and servants, were gathered in the great room of an inn in southwest London. Billy Costello was a knight, an aide to Alan. The men had assembled there to decide how to handle their request that King John yield more freedom to them to allow them more influence in the government.

Alan had called the meeting. He was the main leader among the barons. All the nobles were camped, along with many of their knights, in nearby areas, here in the southwest area of London. Some of them had been there for several weeks and others had come in recently.

At one point, a few days ago, they had made a deliberate march into the city, in parade form, partly to show their strength and partly to show that they meant business. They wanted changes made, and made now!

Most of the Londoners were friendly to their cause. They had opened the city gates to allow them to march in and parade. Many city folk lined the short parade route and showed their agreement with the efforts of the barons. The Londoners also wanted to see changes made. They, too, were suffering under the rule of King John.

The barons were ready to demand, to insist, that King John grant to them their rights, rights that had been given them a hundred years ago, in 1100, when King Henry had ascended the throne. That hundred year-old document contained the wording that spelled out their rights. It was known as the **Charter of Liberties**. It was also called the **Coronation Charter** because it happened when King Henry was crowned.

Alan Basset's special group had formed themselves into a committee, a committee that would conduct negotiations with the King. It was composed of twenty-three barons with Alan as the chairman.

"Now, men," said Thomas Basset, brother of Alan, "we've talked about this for months. Actually, some of us began discussing this more than a year ago. And, it's been a burden on all of us for years. Now is the time for us to make some changes, to have our rights restored."

"I'm not ready to make any changes," firmly stated Adam Hugh, turning away from the fireplace and looking at Alan and Thomas. "I'm a conservative and a loyal subject. We need strong leadership and our King gives us that. We should be happy with the *status quo.*"

"Yes, by God!" said Alan, standing up and thundering, looking fiercely towards Adam. "He gives us strong leadership, a leadership that is too damned strong! He's infringed on our rights. We must demand that our rights be returned to us. I repeat what I said earlier, **we are not slaves!**"

"He's not making us slaves," insisted Adam, "he's just performing his God-given duties. He has knowledge that we don't have and he can act for us in a beneficial way."

"Hold on there," replied Alan, angrily. "You make us out to be little children with our father, the King, telling us what to do all of the time. Well, let me tell you, my hearty, I'm not a child, I'm a grown man. And I'm a smart grown man who doesn't need to be led by the nose."

"I'm older than the King," he went on, still full of heat and anger. "How can I let someone, who is younger than me, act as my father? We get enough of that with the Church. There, we've got to call the priests *father*. Ha! That's pretty stupid." He walked around the table.

"Here I am," he continued, "almost fifty years old and I'm expected, by some thirty-year-old youngster, who is just out of the seminary, to call him **my father**? Ho, Ho, Ho. How ridiculous can you get? How stupid can you be? Don't put me in your class of dummies! Not-so-bright people who are willing to be led around like babies!"

"Let me be a loyal subject to my King," he added, "but not a slave to his direction and leadership. I'll fight for him when he's right but when he's wrong, I'll insist that he needs to change courses."

"Well, sire," said Adam, sneeringly, with a tone of mockery in his voice, "what you say seems to be a new concept. You sound like you want to be free to do whatever you wish! Where did that thought come from?"

"That thought comes right from King Henry!" said Alan, strongly and decisively, while looking sternly at Adam Hugh. "For many, many years we had King Henry's Charter. That's not a new concept, as you want to say. That Charter gave us many, many rights—a hundred years ago! And King John has abused our rights, the rights that are stated in that Charter!"

"The proposal that we have given the King to consider," he said, "is fair and just and follows King Henry's Charter. There's no reason why so many of our rights have been taken away from us."

Alan, trying to regain his calm nature, walked over to the fireplace and poked some of the wood. The other men talked among themselves; some sat in silence. But they all agreed with Alan. Adam stood to one side, staring fixedly at nothing in particular.

Just then, a messenger arrived from King John. Four aides accompanied him. He came up to Alan and handed him a flat pouch. Alan took out a parchment from inside it and began to read.

"My friends," said Alan, somewhat triumphantly, "the King will meet us tomorrow. He will meet us at Runnymede meadow at one hour before noon. He is willing to discuss our proposals with us."

"His message says that he is bringing our brother, Peter Fitz Herbert," he added. "I think that means the King is ready to grant our wishes. Certainly, he is ready to parlay."

"Let me see that message," said Adam. Alan handed him the parchment.

Adam closely read the document but he said nothing. He handed it back to Alan. Alan handed it to John Marshal who read it and passed it on to Thomas Bennet. He read it and passed it on to the others. As each one read it, they looked up to Alan and smiled.

"Men," said Alan, "I think we've won this argument. I feel sure that the King will renew the rights we formerly had. He will agree to the proposals that we have made to him and he will reduce his almighty power somewhat."

"What we need to do," he added, "is to be vigilant. He may come with more iron chains for us, but we should hold firm in our desire for more autonomy. We cannot allow ourselves to weaken. We're not against our Lord, the King. We only wish to not be treated as slaves."

"Hurrah!" shouted Thomas. And, most of the others shouted along with him. "We are loyal subjects," said Thomas, as he rose to speak, "and we want to help the King rule the country. But we want to be looked on with favor, not to be treated as common men."

"I am going back to my tent," said Alan. "Early tomorrow morning we will ride over to Runnymede and meet with the King. That place is two miles East of here, on the south bank of the Thames. We'll form our group near my tent-site. I'll lead the way." He looked over the group to see if there was any dissent; there was none.

"All right. Billy, let us go," he said, as he turned to Billy and prepared to leave.

"One other thing, men," he said as approached the doorway to the exterior, "each of you should bring at least fifty men, to show our strength and to show that we will not back down. There should be no fight, no battle, but prepare yourselves anyway, as if there will be a fight. We must be prepared. We must be strong. We must show our strength."

The next morning dawned sunny and bright. The nobles gathered near Alan's tent-site and twenty minutes later they were at Runnymede meadow.

Alan Basset spoke to his brother, Thomas, then to John Marshal, and Philip Daubney. They formed into a small group. Billy Costello stood alongside Alan. The other nobles had knights and squires nearby to aid them.

Adam Hugh did not go with Alan's group. He was not seen after the afternoon meeting in the tavern. He later appeared with the King's courtiers. Perhaps he had been the king's spy in Alan's group. Whispers abounded, conjecturing that he had been planted in Alan's group, that he really was an informer for the King, that he was not trustworthy.

By mid-morning, some of the King's men arrived and set up a long table and a large chair for the King to use. Other chairs were placed at the sides of the table.

As the table and chairs were being set up, one of the King's men brought in a man. "Here's your fellow," he said, as he handed over Peter Fitz Herbert.

"Peter! Peter!" shouted Alan, as Billy hurried over to walk alongside this new arrival. He supported him on one side as Peter slowly made his way to Alan's arms.

"What did they do to you, my dear friend, Peter?" cried Alan. He could see that Peter had been mistreated, possibly tortured "By God, they'll pay for this," he growled as he looked toward the King's men, who were returning to their side. They heard what Alan said.

Billy helped Peter to a chair at the table. He found a blanket and folded it into a cushion to make Peter's seat more comfortable.

"Yes," said Peter, to Alan, "they certainly banged me around a lot. I'm not complete, not one-hundred percent, I'll tell you. They starved me, too. I haven't had much to eat for the past ten days or so. Actually I've lost track of time."

"Oh, those dirty rats!" exclaimed Alan. "There's too much of that torture going on. We'll get you well, we'll restore your health, believe me. And that kind of mistreatment will only steel our will to getting what we want!"

Billy went to Alan's horse and opened a saddlebag. He brought back some bread and cheese along with a bottle of good wine. Peter devoured everything put in front of him and he seemed to grow stronger right before their eyes.

Just before twelve noon, the King rode up, accompanied by a troop of at least ten knights. As he approached the table, Alan signaled to some of his men who were on horseback. They formed a line behind Alan's group. More horsemen filed in behind the first line. Eventually, they were five lines deep and about twenty men in a line.

The King's men helped him to dismount. He walked over to the large high-backed chair at the table.

Alan Basset, Thomas Basset, John Marshal, and Philip Daubney, walked forward to the table and took seats opposite King John. Peter Fitz Herbert sat on one side of Alan and Billy Costello sat on the other.

Adam Hugh took a chair at the end of the table. As each man took his seat, he bowed to the King. A scribe sat at the King's left hand. Alan shot a cold, hard glance at Adam Hugh, who elected to not meet Alan's gaze.

"My worthy nobles," began King John, in a somewhat friendly, mollifying manner, "I came here today to comment on the proposals that you recently sent to me. They are not suitable and I refuse to honor them, of course. If you wish otherwise, now is the time to say so."

Alan stood up, bowed, and said: "Your Highness, we have proposed only those rights that have been in effect since King Henry's Coronation Charter. We ask that you abide by the stipulations that are in that Charter—those have been our rights for many, many years. There is nothing new in our proposals. We, your loyal subjects, are asking that you abide by the policy of this realm for all these years, since King Henry. We humbly ask for your indulgence." He remained standing while this message sank into King John's brain.

"What is this King Henry's Coronation Charter?" asked King John, acting a bit displeased.

"Here is a copy of it," said Alan, quickly, as he took a parchment from his handbag and handed it to the scribe who, in turn, handed it to the King. The scribe and the King looked at it together. The scribe helped the King to read it.

"I was not aware of this Charter," said King John. Either he was making an excuse or he really had never seen it. Alan was sure that the King knew about the Charter and was avoiding it. The King could not have suspected that Alan would have the Charter with him, ready to confront King John with it, right then and there.

"I need to take a recess before we go any further," he said. "You have brought up a new subject for me to consider. This should have been considered before now."

Alan simply bowed in response. Of course, the King should have considered the Coronation Charter before this meeting, long before this meeting. If he had been a wise king, he would have used this Charter in his deliberations. Alan suspected that King John simply wanted to rule by his own means and not refer to underlying rights that appeared in earlier documents.

Several attendants turned the King's chair away from the table and then the King, the scribe, and four or five courtiers formed a circle and discussed the Charter. They talked at some length, occasionally looking at Alan and his team members. After about thirty minutes, the scribe began to write on a new parchment. The King and his advisors continuously commented to the scribe as he wrote.

At one point, the King turned to Alan and asked: "You will not change your demands to your sovereign?"

"No, sire," answered Alan, quickly and firmly. "We are your loyal subjects but we are not slaves. We have asked only for what has been guaranteed to us since King Henry! And, we are prepared to help you grant our requests."

The King turned back to the scribe and to his advisors for more discussion. Alan had just shown some muscle. The King could see the 5-men-deep lines of horsemen behind Alan. It may have passed through the King's mind that Alan and the barons could, at that very moment, just run right through the King and his courtiers and slay them all.

Finally, after more than two hours, near mid-afternoon, the King signed his name to the parchment. The scribe carried the signed document to Alan. He and his men studied it. It granted them everything that they had proposed!

"This is well-done," said Alan, as he stood and bowed to the King. His key men rose to stand, too. He wanted to be courteous when he spoke. "We are pleased with Your Majesty's efforts and we are ready to return to our lands. We remain loyal subjects to Your Majesty. We ask your scribe to make several copies, so we can have them to distribute among our fellow nobles." He and his teammates remained standing.

King John watches the prepartation
of the Magna Carta

The scribe sat and made another three copies of the new Charter and handed them to Billy who relayed them to Alan. Alan looked them over to see that they were identical with the first issue.

While the copies were being made, The King arose, nodded his assent, and turned to go. His horse was brought to him. He mounted and rode off, almost nonchalantly, without even a wave to Alan and his group of nobles. Adam Hugh rode off in the King's group.

Alan and his men stood there, at the table, staring after their sovereign, waiting for him to go out of sight. They were glad for the victory and were hoping that he would not forget to honor this new Charter, this Magna Carta. If he didn't keep his word, there would be a much more serious uprising, an event that might tear apart this noble land.

But, whether the King waved to them or not, whether the King was sincere or not, they had his signature on the document, on the Great Charter, the Magna Carta, the document that restored their rights as noblemen.

As the king rode out of sight, Alan turned to Thomas and, with a wide smile and a face full of happiness, said: "We've won a great victory here on this gentle field of Runnymede. We have rights now that had been taken from us and they have been returned. This gives us the powers that we should have and that we should have had all along. We are free men again, no longer slaves to our king."

'Yes," said Thomas, standing back and saluting his brother, "We are whole again. King John has proved to be a noble King. He saw the benefits of our loyalty. And, he also saw our strength. Several times, he looked at our horsemen, lined up and ready for whatever would come up. I'm sure that the King's not as happy about our having some say in the governing of this great land, this England, but we know that is the rightful way to go. Rulers often try to take too much power; this is one time that we've stopped that. We have a voice and we are an important part of this government."

"Future generations of English men will honor this day," said Alan, "this 15th of June in the year of our Lord 1215. Billy, write down some notes of this happening today. It's a rare day for all of us, for all of us who call ourselves Englishmen."

Billy, with parchment and pen and stylus, did just that. The men gathered up their belongings and rode back to where their troops were encamped. Over the next several days they would ride off to their own lands with the glorious word that their freedoms had been restored.

As Alan rode, with his troops, back to his home, he said to Billy, who was riding alongside him: "This Magna Carta is more important than we think just now. It will form a new basis for free men and it will be copied by future governments as yet unknown."

"Yes, sire," said Billy, happy to have been part of this great event.

"See to it that our men are ready to march back home early tomorrow," said Alan. "I will meet you later at my tent site and we'll go over our plans."

"Yes, sire, I will do just as you say," replied Billy. They parted. Alan rode off and Billy walked away towards the well to get a cold drink of water. But when he'd gone only about ten steps, and was about to reach the bucket of water, he woke up. And, there was Thalia and the good doctor smiling at him.

"You must have had a fantastic trip," exclaimed Thalia, "We could tell that you were deeply involved with whatever you were doing. What was it?"

"It was the Magna Carta," said Billy, triumphantly, as he sat up, "the signing of the Magna Carta, at Runnymede, long ago, in 1215."

"I'm so thirsty," said Billy, and Thalia hastened to get him a glass of water.

"Thanks," he said, "it was wonderful. "That's how my dream ended. I was about to get a drink of water because I was so thirsty!"

"The scribe was using a quill-point pen to write with," said Billy. "It was similar to what we use today. Imagine that, no advancement in 600 years!" he laughed.

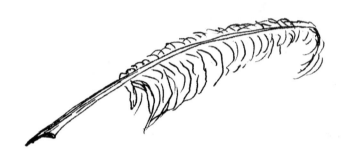

"I was with Alan Basset, a leader of the barons who rose up against King John," said Billy, excitedly. "Alan and the barons wanted to get King John to change his ruling edicts and grant certain rights to the barons, rights that they'd earlier had but King John had taken away from them."

Doctor Dulcamara was taking notes as he listened. Billy told them of the meeting at Runnymede and the arrival of the king and the signing of the Magna Carta.

"Oh, it was wonderful," said Billy, as he spoke of the details of that meeting in June 1215 in England.

The doctor kept scribbling away and soon had three pages of notes. Earlier, he had taken Billy's temperature, his blood pressure, and jotted down other signs of his condition. Billy was none the worse for the experience and he was exuberant, truly excited about this first major time that he'd been under hypnosis.

"When can we do it again?" asked Billy. "I'm ready for another adventure."

"Well, this one went very well," said Dr. Dulcamara. "So, let's plan for another one next week."

"I want to get in on the act," said Thalia. "Can't you put me in line for a session?"

"Of course, my dear," replied the doctor. "You know that my research should include females as well as males. So, you can be the subject on the next trial or the one after that. I think that for the next trial, we should do Billy again, and following that, we can plan to do you."

"Oh, goody!" exclaimed Thalia. "This is such a wonderful idea, I just can't wait to get started. I'll be on pins and needles until my turn comes."

Chapter 3

Julius Caesar Dies

"Hello," said Dr. Dulcamara, to Billy and his wife, Thalia, as they came in mid-afternoon, to prepare for another test using the doctor's increasing ability to study them while they were under an hypnotic spell.

"Hello, Doctor," said Billy and Thalia, in unison.

"We're all set to undergo another test," said Billy. "Thalia has been cramming me full of information about the death of Julius Caesar."

"In 44 B. C.," interjected Thalia, enthusiastically, "Billy now knows the complete story and we hope it will mature in his dream, while he is under the hypnotic spell."

"Well, I hope so, too," replied the doctor. "That will be another success for me. Each time he, or you, can dream that you are present during some long-ago historical event, and feel that you are really there—that will be a success!"

"I am so glad that you and Billy are willing to work with me on this project," he continued. "It will result in great success for this unusual research that I am performing. I believe that I'm the only doctor that is doing this type of investigation. This is the New Frontier in medical research!"

"And, we're glad to be part of it," stated Billy, proud of his participation in this medical project. "It is doing a lot for me. When I dream about the death of Caesar, as I hope to do this afternoon, it really teaches me a direct lesson from history. To imagine that I am right there, at the time of the important event—well, nothing can top that!"

"You're right, Billy," responded the doctor. "Actually being present while the historical event is taking place, is a rare privilege indeed."

"But," he added, "let's get prepared for today. Are you ready or do you wish more time."

"No, no," said Billy, as he took a seat on the couch. "I'm ready, as ready as I could expect to be."

"All right," said the doctor. "Let's have you lie back on the couch and close your eyes momentarily. Thalia," he looked to her, "do you have anything you want to say to Billy before he leaves us?"

"No," laughed Thalia, "I've pretty well filled him with info about Caesar, so he's all prepared and ready to go off to 44 B.C."

"All right, Billy," said the doctor, as he became more serious and attentive to his work. "You can open your eyes and look closely at my watch. It is gradually and gently swaying," he said, speaking in low, sonorous tones. All was quiet; you could almost hear the nearly-silent ticking of the watch.

"Watch it sway and," in very low tones, almost a whisper, "all of a sudden, you are not with us." At that moment Billy's eyes closed and he fell back on the sofa.

Thalia helped the doctor to bring Billy's legs up on the sofa and put some cushions behind his shoulders, to make him more comfortable.

Billy found himself on a street in ancient Rome. He was part of a group of aides and servants who were accompanying Julius Caesar to the Senate.

"Oh, Mighty Caesar," said the boy who was offering a basket of fruit to the man who was considering declaring himself Emperor. Julius Caesar, the head of the Roman Empire, was walking along the street, accompanied by several of his aides, one of whom was Billy Costello.

"Billy," said Caesar, as he nodded to the boy with the fruit, "take some of that fruit, some of those dried plums especially, and hold them for me until later. Give him some coins—I will take nothing without paying for it. Make sure that he is not underpaid."

Billy buys fruit at Caesar's directiion

P Nancarrow

"Yes, sir," said Billy, snappily, as he picked out several pieces of fruit and put them into a small bag he was carrying. He handed the boy some coins.

Caesar, Billy, and the others were slowly walking from Caesar's house to the Senate chambers. It was rumored that an ally of Caesar was going to nominate him to be Emperor. Billy, who was a low-level aide, was someone who ran errands for Caesar and his household. In addition, he retrieved scrolls from the library, delivered messages to friends, and other simple chores. He was walking along with the group, ready to do any service that was asked of him.

An old man stepped in front of Caesar. "Beware," he said, "this is the Ides of March!"

One of Caesar's friends quickly stepped in front to push the old man out of the way, but Caesar raised his hand—and everyone stopped right there! When Caesar raised a hand, it was a signal for everyone to stop whatever they were doing, and pay attention, to listen to what Caesar was about to say.

"Nay," said Caesar, compassionately and imperiously, "let him be. He has every right to speak to me."

"Old man," he said to the fellow, "it's true that this is the Ides of March, and I was warned some time ago to be careful on this day. But it has come," he paused to look about and to smile to the onlookers, "and no evil has happened to me."

"Aye, sire," replied the old man, speaking very seriously, "it has come, but it has not gone! There is still time left in the day. Be careful."

"I thank you for your concern in my welfare," said Caesar, rather expansively, "but Heaven has guarded me so far and I will rely on the Gods to continue to protect me. They must have a divine plan for me."

"May it be so," replied the old man, as he stepped back into the crowd. He was soon swallowed up among the throng.

"Billy," said Caesar.

"Yes, sire," answered Billy.

"Give that old man some coins," said Caesar. "He looks very gaunt, he must be hungry. He needs food and he should have money to buy it. Some day I may be old and hungry and then, maybe some man will give me coins to buy food."

Billy dived into the crowd and found the old man. He offered him enough money to buy bread and cheese. But, the old man would not take the money.

"Your master is on his last legs," said the old man, with a doomsday mien. "He will not return this way. His walking on this Earth is nearly done. He is now walking to his Death! Beware!"

Billy stepped back. He looked carefully at the old man. What did this ancient, thin, gaunt fellow know? Did he have a magic connection with the Gods, a connection that allowed him to foretell the events of the day? Could he actually foretell the death of Mighty Caesar?

"How do you know this, sir?" asked Billy.

"You're too young to understand, my boy," replied the old man, as he laid his hand on Billy's shoulder. "There is much mystery in the world. You must get older and older just to learn a little part of it."

Then the old man turned away. Another man near him said to Billy: "That old man is a soothsayer. He has great knowledge about the mysteries of life. He can predict the future. Believe in him."

Billy shook his head, knowing that he did not understand the ways of old people. He trotted off to catch up with Caesar and his group. Caesar stopped so often to talk to the people, that he was not very far ahead. Billy was beside him within a few strides. He watched Caesar smile at everyone, a direct smile that beamed goodwill onto them. He noticed that the people all tried to touch Caesar or his garments as if there were magic there—and that magic could help them.

This seemingly leisurely walk that Caesar was making to meet with the Senators was really a triumphant walk. Caesar was an astute politician. He wanted the Senators to know that the populace loved him, that the people felt honored just to be standing next to this great man, even just to touch his garments. In fact, every time that Caesar walked out in public, it became a triumphal walk. The people loved him and everyone wanted to walk with him.

Eventually, Caesar and his group, including Billy, arrived at the Senate building and began to climb the short flight of steps to go into the deliberating chambers.

Meanwhile, back at Julius Caesar's palace, his wife, Calpurnia, was out of sorts. She had suddenly become nervous. She went from this room to that room, picking up something, and then laying it down.

"Madame," said her maid. "Come and sit here and I'll bring you some tea."

"No, not just yet," replied Calpurnia. "It's just that I don't know if I want to sit down or stand up. I might seem to be a bit on edge, but I am worried about my husband. He was so cheerful when he left here an hour ago to go to the Senate, but I have suddenly had this overwhelming foreboding. Just in the past few minutes, I have a feeling of dread."

"I just can't get this strange feeling out of my mind," she said, as she nervously rolled the sleeve from her garment in her hands. She dropped the sleeve and walked into the next room, the maid following.

Calpurnia looked up at the ceiling. At that moment she heard a loud Crash!

"Did you hear that?" she whirled to her maid.

"No, Madame," replied the maid, quietly, "I heard nothing."

"You heard nothing!?" Calpurnia seemed dumbfounded.

"You heard nothing?" she repeated, almost as a demand. She couldn't believe that the maid had heard nothing.

"No, Madame, in all truth, I heard nothing," replied the maid, with a slight shiver.

"Something has happened to Caesar!" screamed Calpurnia. "He's been set upon. He's been attacked. He's fighting back against them. Who are they?"

She strode into the other room.

"Get my wrap," she commanded to the maid, as she turned suddenly, "I must go to the Senate at once, right now!"

Meanwhile, Billy, only a few paces behind Caesar, had accompanied him up the steps, and into the Senate building. Some of the senators rose from their seats as Caesar appeared in the entrance. Some came to greet him.

Being the good politician that he was, he reached out to clasp their extended arms. He welcomed them and they welcomed him. There were smiles all around.

But, suddenly, an arm appeared behind him. He didn't see it. It held a long-bladed knife. The man behind, holding the knife, pushed Billy out of the way. "Here's a greeting from Tillius Cimber!" he cried, as he plunged his knife into Caesar's back, between the shoulder blades.

Caesar staggered but did not go down. He turned to stare at Cimber. His gaze was fierce and defiant. As he turned to the front, he cried: "This is violence!" and tried to protect himself.

Just then, Casca thrust his knife toward Caesar's throat. Caesar lifted his arm to defend himself, but that left his front open and others began to attack him.

Suddenly, he saw Brutus preparing to do his part in the assassination. He looked at Brutus, his protégé, and said, almost resignedly, "And, you, too, my child."

Brutus, with a grim countenance, pushed forward his blade into Caesar's chest. Caesar wilted before the man who he had considered to be as his own son.

When he realized that Brutus, practically his own flesh and blood, was part of this attack, Caesar lost all resistance. He brought up his toga and covered his face, as four, five, six more conspirators plunged their knives into his body. He fell at the feet of Pompey's statue.

Billy, who was just behind Caesar, had been pushed out of the way. He lost his balance and he fell, but he quickly regained his feet.

But he was too far from the action. He could do nothing to help. Those big, strong men assassinating Caesar were like an impenetrable wall, surrounding their victim. No one could get close enough, quickly enough to help Caesar. It was all over in less than two minutes.

Caesar was dead! And, Billy knew it. What should he do now? Would they look to slay him? He was unimportant, just a little peanut who didn't count, so he was sure that they had no interest in him.

He was not excessively brave but he was not timid. However, he did have good sense. If he couldn't help the situation, he should get out of there. He began to step backward towards the entrance and then down the steps of the building.

He quickly turned and began to race towards Caesar's palace. About a hundred yards before he reached the home, he met Calpurnia and her maid.

Calpurnia was blindly rushing towards the Senate building, with her maid and other retainers in tow, all trying to keep up with her headlong dash to be with her husband. The many people crowding the street impeded them.

"My Madame, my Madame," said Billy, as he came face-to-face with his mistress. "Please do not go further. There is nothing you can do to help. I beg you to return home."

"Oh, Billy," said Calpurnia, as she paused in her flight, "tell me what is going on? I have fears, I have dreadful fears! I fear that something terrible has happened."

"Madame," said Billy, trying to sound less alarming, "there's been a fight, an altercation. Some people have been hurt," he did not want to tell her that Caesar had been killed, "and I came to tell you that much. Please go back home and the news will get to you very quickly."

Billy did not want to be the one to give her the news of her husband's death, even though he knew that Mighty Caesar, the Great Caesar, was dead. Also, it was not his position in the household.

The street was filling with even more citizens. There was alarm and rumors began: "Caesar is Dead!" There was frenzy and shouting and no one seemed to know where to go or to gather, to gain some sense out of what was happening. It was impossible to make headway in any direction. Calpurnia realized that.

"All right," said Calpurnia, to no one in particular, "I'll go back home and await the news." She said this in a low tone, as if there was no more intensity left in her.

She turned, and with her servants and maid, slowly dragged herself back home. In reality, she was unwilling to go home, but she realized that she might be in terrible danger herself and the wise thing to do was to be at home rather than out here in the street in the midst of the milling crowd.

Arriving home, her maid handed a glass of wine to this distraught lady. Very soon, a messenger came in and spoke to the Guard Captain. Billy knew what the news was and he watched as the Guard Captain walked over Calpurnia and bowed. On his knees, he spoke quietly to Caesar's wife.

Calpurnia buried her face in her hands. Just then, her sister and some other relatives came rushing into the room and went to comfort Calpurnia.

The Guard Captain came over to Billy and the others and told them they should leave the room. As they filed out, Billy walked off towards the right. There was a drinking fountain and he stopped for a drink of water.

A drinking fountain! In 44 B. C.? No way. Suddenly, Billy realized that it was Thalia, offering him a glass of water, just as he was waking from his duties at Caesar's home.

"Ha, Ha!" laughed Billy, as he rose up from a lying position, to sit upright on the doctor's couch and sip the water from the glass that Thalia had handed to him.

"Wow! What a dream!" Billy exclaimed. "I was right there! Right there when Caesar was assassinated." He leaned back on the couch.

"Wow! Wow! Wow!" he exclaimed. "That was so real! Boy oh Boy, I saw everything and I was right there, participating in everything that was going on. It was terrific!"

He was beside himself with glee. Thalia, smiling, happy, sat next to him. Dr. Dulcamara, with his ever-present note pad sat near, scribbling notes in a rapid fashion.

"It was really true, authentic?" asked Thalia, excitedly.

"Oh, yes, yes, yes," said Billy. "My goodness, I can't tell you how real that was."

Thalia and the doctor pumped Billy for all of the details of his trip back to 44 B.C. when Caesar was assassinated. They were astounded at what all Billy had to tell them. He described the event in detail.

It is one thing to pick up a book and read about an historical event and it's a different thing to be present at the event, taking in everything that was going on at that time.

Being present provides a reality that cannot be found when someone tells about a happening, telling the story from hearsay, from reports made at that special time. Actually being there is a real-life type of experience. That's what Dr. Dulcamara's experiments provided to Billy and Thalia.

Chapter 4

Cleopatra

"Now, Thalia," said Dr. Dulcamara, "you've seen your husband, Billy, have a session with me, and you know what to expect. It will be the same with you as it was with Billy."

"Yes, doctor," replied Thalia, "I've watched closely and I'm sure I can undergo your treatment as well as he did."

"All right," said the doctor. "Here's what I want you to do." He described the treatment session, that he would hypnotize her and she would sleep for about twenty or thirty minutes. Then she'd awaken and tell him what she had experienced.

"Do you have an historic subject picked out?" he asked.

"Yes," she replied, eagerly. "I'm hoping to connect with Cleopatra, the Queen of Egypt."

"Oh, that's such a good subject," said Billy, as he prepared to sit and observe his wife while she was asleep.

"I've wanted to be there at a critical time, when she dies," said Thalia, "when she commits suicide."

"That sounds terribly tragic," said the doctor.

"Yes, it is," replied Thalia, reflectively, "it was too bad for her, and she only thirty-nine years old. Not even middle-aged as years go. She'd had such bad luck, first with Julius Caesar by whom she had a son, named Caesarian, and with Marc Anthony, who was the father of three of her children."

"Now, Julius and Marc were dead," she added "and Marc's conqueror, Augustus, was coming to make a prisoner of her. She had no one left to protect her."

"Well, let's hope that your dreams materialize," said the doctor. "Are you ready?"

"Oh, yes," exclaimed Thalia. "I've been ready for two weeks." They all had a good laugh at that.

Thalia lay back on the couch and Dr. Dulcamara began to hypnotize her. She quickly passed out and was in dreamland within a few seconds.

Thalia was one of several maids, women-in-waiting who attended Cleopatra. Thalia, though only a maid, was very aware of what was going on. Just then, Cornelius, a close advisor to the Queen, came into the room. He walked over and stood next to Thalia. They seemed to have been friends for some time.

"Cornelius," said Thalia, almost whispering, "you always know what's happening and now there appears to be a critical event shaping up. What's the explanation?"

"Well," said Cornelius, "it goes back a long ways. You may recall that the Macedonian, Alexander, conquered Egypt about three hundred years ago. But he died soon after and his kingdoms were awarded to his generals. It was General Ptolemy who became the ruler of Egypt."

"And," he went on, "Ptolemy was a very smart man. He changed very little about Egypt; he kept the same gods, the same religion, and almost all of the same culture. He did update some things and promoted the beautiful library in the new city of Alexandria. The library has over seven hundred thousand scrolls in it. In fact, all ships that come into the harbor are examined for books and if any book is found, that is not already in the Great Library, it is confiscated and soon appears in the Library."

"I didn't know that about the confiscation," replied Thalia. "I did know that we have the finest library in the world."

"To continue," said Cornelius, "Cleopatra is descended from Ptolemy and an Egyptian lady. She was in line to rule Egypt but she had to work her way through a lot of intrigue before gaining the crown at the tender age of eighteen. She was young in body but she was very wise in mind. And, she still is young and wise."

"And," he went on, "when she did become Queen, she needed protection for her country from the Big Bear, the Roman Empire. She was a good politician and she soon realized that she needed to form an alliance with Rome, actually with Julius Caesar, the main man in Rome."

"Caesar came to Egypt," he added, "and those two met as equals, even though both knew that Caesar was the bigger equal. Cleopatra was not without brains and body—a lot of charm. She called Caesar Horus, the king of the Egyptian gods, and she named herself Hathor, the Egyptian goddess. Caesar accepted this other religion and did not insist that Egypt bow down to his gods."

"She soon became pregnant and gave birth to a child, aptly named Caesarion. That, she was sure, would give Egypt the protection of the mighty Romans, of mighty Caesar himself. It was a very wise, a very diplomatic thing that she did for her country."

"Then, Fate stepped in," he said. "When his son, Caesarion, was born, Cleopatra came under the protective umbrella of Julius Caesar. But, he was assassinated by his own people and—*poof!*—there went the protection that Caesar could personally supply to Cleopatra."

"When Caesar was killed," he continued, "three rulers gained control in Rome. They were Augustus, Marc Anthony, and another guy who soon opted out. Marc Anthony was given the Eastern Empire which included Egypt and Augustus was given the Western Empire."

"Now, Cleopatra had to make a new alliance for the protection of her country," he said. "And, Marc Anthony was the new man to protect her and Egypt. She had three children by Marc Anthony, two girls and a boy, as you know. So, she had a new protector and all was well."

"But," he said, sadly, "Marc Anthony and Augustus had a falling out and recently Augustus beat Anthony in a major battle. To avoid capture, Anthony committed suicide, dying in Cleopatra's arms, so I've been told."

"Now, at this very moment, Augustus is coming to make a prisoner of our Queen, Cleopatra," he said, wiping a tear from his eye. "And, my Queen, my Dear Queen, is distraught. She must make some important decisions and quickly. What will she do next? What should she do next? I don't know."

"Oh, look," said Thalia, "she is asking Iris for something."

"Dear Iris," said Cleopatra, to her favorite lady-in-waiting, "go to Demetrius and bring me the gold box that he has for me. He is in the flower house."

"Yes, mistress," replied Iris, as she curtsied, stepped backward and quickly went out through the purple doors.

"Look," said Thalia to a nearby maid, "did you see? She's sent Iris away on some errand."

"Yes," replied her friend. "Iris is her favorite. She is probably going to get something for our mistress."

Thalia and the other maids stood inside the entrance to Cleopatra's bedroom. They could see everything that was going on. Their main purpose was to help their mistress in anything that was needed; a wave of Cleopatra's hand brought several of her maids quickly to her side. They were required to be as quiet and discreet as possible.

Iris was young, barely fifteen, but she had been a maid to Cleopatra since she was seven or eight years old. She now walked quickly to the flower house and there she saw Demetrius pruning some small shrubs.

"My mistress wants the gold box," said Iris, firmly, to Demetrius. In a sisterly way, she liked Demetrius but he was strict and stern and old and grouchy. About forty-five years old, he had studied many of the sciences, especially astronomy and anatomy. Besides his work in the flower house, he also helped in the animal house where all kinds of animals, even snakes, were kept. He was very accurate in anything that he did.

Demetrius looked sharply at Iris, almost as if he was looking straight through her. A slight shiver ran up the spine of the frightened woman. He did look fierce, she could see. But he was not mean-looking. He was strict with everyone, but he was kind, too.

"Why does she want it?" he asked. He knew what was in the box and he was sure that some terrible event was in store when that special box was taken from him. He'd been required to prepare it. It contained a snake, an asp, a type of Egyptian cobra. Someone was due to die and he knew it. Could it be his Queen?

"She didn't say," replied Iris, as she leaned over to smell some of the flowers. She seemed unconcerned with the importance of her errand.

"That's it, then?" he asked. "She just told you to come and get it?"

"Yes," replied Iris, "and I am to take it to her. Those were my orders. That was what my mistress said."

"Alright," replied Demetrius, soberly. He knew that Iris knew nothing, that she had no idea that she would be carrying Death-in-a-Box with her. "You wait right here. Don't go anywhere. I'll be back in a few minutes."

He turned and carefully stepped around several pots of plants and disappeared through a small doorway. In about three minutes, he came back with a small box. It was about a foot long and several inches wide and deep. It was covered with gold leaf. A symbol of a snake was on the top. There was a metal clasp at the middle, keeping the lid closed.

"Keep this top upright," instructed Demetrius. "Do not, I repeat, do not, drop this box. Hold it tightly. Absolutely, do not let it fall. Never let this clasp come loose. If you let it fall, it would be better that you had killed yourself!"

Iris trembled as he said these words. He was forceful and he wanted to impress on her the terrible responsibility that she was about to undertake. He knew what was inside the box, but she had no idea. The difference in knowledge was vast.

Demetrius helped her to get a firm grip on the small box, to hold it against her breast, with her left arm completely wrapped around it.

"Now walk carefully," he reminded her. "Watch where you're going. When you come to any steps or stairs, be careful how you use them."

"Yes, sir," replied Iris, feeling stuffed full of advice, "I'll be careful, I'll walk carefully."

"Your life depends upon it!" commanded Demetrius.

Another shiver went up her spine as she carefully stepped away from him, and began her short walk back to her mistress' bedroom.

"Here she comes," said Thalia to Cornelius. "She's got a box with her. It looks like it's covered with gold."

"Yes," he replied. "I wonder what's in it."

They stepped aside as Iris walked between them into the bedroom where her mistress reclined on a couch, a couch with many pillows.

Iris walked up to her mistress and handed her the box.

"Thank you, Iris," said Cleopatra. "You may go over there."

Cleopatra, smiling, but preparing to die

Iris walked over to a corner of the room and sat on some very large pillows, near some of the other maids. She kept her mistress in sight, ready to respond to any signal from her.

Cleopatra held the box on her lap. She knew what was in it and she knew what she intended to do, actually what she knew she had to do. Her gaze went up and she looked out beyond the balcony towards the far horizon. The sky was clear and blue.

Cleopatra had come to a crisis point. She was the Queen of Egypt. She was the mother of Julius Caesar's son Caesarion and she had borne three children of Marc Anthony.

But now, Caesar was long dead, fourteen years ago, murdered in the Roman Senate. Marc Anthony had died by his own hand last week. Today, the twelfth of August, was her day to die.

But why should she, the Queen of Egypt die? She was only thirty-nine and in good health. She had many productive years ahead of her.

Ah! Devilish Politics. In her world, Fate had intervened when she had chosen her protectors. Marc Anthony was gone and no longer protecting her. His conqueror, Augustus, was about to enter Alexandria and make her his prisoner.

A prisoner! She winced as she said that word half aloud. "A prisoner! No, never. No, never!"

She could see herself, in chains, maybe naked or in rags, being paraded before the populace—the jeering populace. Being treated like an animal, screamed at, spit upon, struck with stones and vegetables. She, the Queen of Egypt—she would never submit to that torture.

"See that," said Thalia. "She looks like she's talking to herself, as if she is recalling her past, as if she is reviewing what should be done."

"Yeah," said Cornelius, "she's in a reverie. She's in a mood, daydreaming, just looking out into the sky and doing some dreaming. Everybody has day-dreams."

"Well," added Thalia, "it looks pretty serious to me. My woman's intuition tells me that she is serious, she is planning something; she's not laughing or singing. She is talking but it's so low I can't hear the words, can you?"

"No, I don't hear anything, she's just talking to herself" said one of the other maids. "Of course, we're too far way. They want it that way. We're not supposed to be close to her. Our job is to keep ourselves constantly ready to help her. Help her with anything she wants."

"True, true," said Thalia. "I'm probably trying to read too much into what she's doing. Whatever she's doing is her business, not any of my business."

"That's the smart way to look at it," said the other maid.

Meanwhile, Cleopatra had shifted the box from her lap to a place beside her left hip. She toyed with the clasp as if to open it, but she did not unclasp it.

She knew the asp was inside ready to inject its venom into whomever came close to it. It had been carefully chosen as a suicide weapon. That snake's venom caused drowsiness and very little pain. The victim fell asleep and never woke up. Such a death was often decreed for royalty.

Again, Cleopatra's thoughts turned to Marc Anthony. He was a good man, a good lover, a strong husband and an able ruler. They made a good pair. But they had lost, lost the naval battle at Actium and a land battle a few weeks ago. Losing the land battle meant that Marc would be taken prisoner and he, too, would be marched in parades before the people. That's why he committed suicide; he would not be taken prisoner by Augustus.

That vision of marching, naked or in rags, before the people, kept recurring to her. She could never be anyone's prisoner. The Queen of Egypt was above that. She shivered as she thought about a parade, with her walking along as a prisoner. Not her, not the Queen of Egypt.

Her Marc Anthony was gone, her Julius Caesar was gone. Both of her protectors, whom she had relied on, were gone, and now it was her turn to go. She slightly opened the lid of the gold box and put her left hand inside. Immediately, she felt the sting of the asp's bite.

"Ah," she exclaimed, and pulled her arm out. She closed the clasp tightly.

"Look," said Thalia, "she just said something."

"I didn't notice," said one of the other maids, somewhat annoyed. "You're paying too much attention to her. Our job is to watch to help her, not read her thoughts."

Thalia said nothing but she couldn't help staring at the beautiful lady on the couch. She just **knew** that something had happened moments before.

Cleopatra, looking satisfied with what she'd done, now waved to Iris.

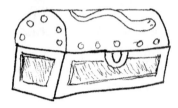

"Take this box back to Demetrius," she said. "And tell him that I wish him well, that I hope that he has all happiness."

"Yes, my mistress," said Iris, dutifully.

"Remember," added Cleopatra, "be very careful with this box and do not drop it and do not open the lid."

"I will do as you say," said Iris, as she took the gold box and wrapped her arm around it. She walked back to the flower house to give it to Demetrius.

Cleopatra's arm began to feel numb and it dropped to her side, then towards the floor. She lay back more fully on the pillows. She was drowsy and felt like sleeping.

She motioned to a guard commander and he went over to her. She spoke to him and he nodded. He came back to the ladies who were in waiting.

"Your mistress has asked me to tell you ladies to leave the room," said the guard officer, as he came over to Thalia and the other maids. "She wants you all to rest. Iris will stay with her mistress."

"Yes, sir," said the maids in unison. As Thalia was leaving the room, she turned to take one more glance back at the Queen of Egypt. Lying on the pillows, one arm dangling down, the Queen, Cleopatra had apparently simply fallen asleep. Iris was standing nearby. Had Thalia fully known, her Queen truly was asleep, a sleep that she would never waken from.

As Thalia left the room and turned a corner in the hallway, she suddenly found herself in the presence of Dr. Dulcamara and her husband, Billy. She was waking up on the couch in the doctor's office. Billy was holding her hand and gently patting her arm.

"I've just seen the most beautiful woman in the world," said Thalia. "In all the world, even in the ancient world."

"Where were you?" asked Billy, excitedly, ignoring the fact that Billy often called **her** the most beautiful woman in the world.

"With Cleopatra in Egypt!" exclaimed Thalia, sitting up.

"And, it was fun?" asked Billy, ever interested in what his wife had just experienced.

"It was a trip!" she said. "There I was, as an attending maid, in the same room as Cleopatra! I can vividly remember what happened when I was there. I feel so privileged just to have been there," she said as the words came tumbling out in a rush.

"One thing I did learn, she was a very wise, a very astute woman. She was not just a *femme fatale*. She was clever and knew how to make alliances, she was equally as smart as Caesar and Marc Anthony. She certainly had more than her share of bad luck!"

She talked with Billy and the doctor for nearly an hour after she woke up. It had been a rare experience for her—

back in Roman times, with Cleopatra, the Queen of Egypt. The story just spilled out of her.

The good doctor had trouble keeping up with her, while he was writing. He took several pages of notes. Thalia was detail oriented and that pleased Doctor Dulcamara. He wanted more and more detail from the patients who were dreaming, dreaming of and experiencing another time-era, when they were under his experimental hypnosis. His goal was to get as much detail as he could about every experience of anyone that he had hypnotized.

Chapter 5

William Tell

"So, tell me," said Thalia to her husband, Billy, as they walked towards the doctor's office, "have you finally decided which historical person you will be with today?"

"It's been a tough decision," said Billy. "I thought that I wanted to be with Robin Hood, but that story about William Tell and his son, years ago in Switzerland, just keeps popping up in my mind. It won't go away."

"Well, lucky you," said Thalia. "You've got something or rather it's got you, so be glad for the connection. As long as it keeps coming back to you, it will probably show up when you're under the doctor's hypnosis."

"That's the right attitude," admitted Billy. "I've got a grip on William Tell and the other subjects can wait for the next time I'm in dreamland."

"Well, here we are at his office," said Thalia, as she knocked on the door.

The door quickly opened and Dr. Dulcamara was standing there, ready to greet them.

"Ah! My favorite couple," he said, as he ushered Thalia and Billy into his office. "Right on time and, I assume, ready with a desire to meet some historical character."

'Yes, sir," said Billy, enthusiastically. "I'm going to try to be with William Tell."

"William Tell, William Tell," mused the doctor. "Let me think about that a moment. Oh, I recall. Wasn't he the Swiss patriot? The hero who shot an apple off his son's head in a village square?"

"That's the one," exclaimed Billy. "I learned about him in grade school. He's been one of my heroes for some years now. I hope I can connect with him since I'd like to be part of that action that occurred so many years ago. Thalia has given me more info about him, so I'm prepared, ready to start whenever you're ready."

"My, oh My," said Dr. Dulcamara, appreciatively. "There's one thing I love about you two. You come here, ready to participate in my experiments. There's no waiting around, there's no dawdling, there's no hesitation. You are ready as soon as you get here. That means a lot to me."

"I try to be ready for you, too," he added. "I know that when you step into my office, you are ready. So, I won't hesitate or dawdle, I'll sit you right down on the sofa, and get us underway."

"Good," said Billy, as he removed his jacket and handed it to Thalia. "Let's go!"

Billy sat on the sofa, reclining against several very large cushions. The doctor asked him to look at a picture on the nearby wall. It was a picture of an apple. Billy smiled. Maybe this would be the apple that William Tell shot off his son's head.

As he was thinking about that and staring at the apple, he suddenly found himself in a rowboat that had just completed a stormy trip across a small lake that was full of high waves and turbulence.

"And, Gessler," shouted William Tell, "that's for you, for your tyrannical laws and terrible treatment of my people." As soon as his feet touched the shore, William Tell had turned and shot an arrow into Gessler's chest.

William Tell had just leaped from the boat that had carried them across the storm-tossed small lake. When they started across the lake, William was in chains but the storm soon grew so menacing, that his chains were removed and his skill with the oars was called on. After all, Gessler and his henchmen didn't want to die just then.

Hermann Gessler, the despotic governor of Uri province in Switzerland, slumped over, gasping for air.

William had skillfully navigated the boat onto the sands of the shore and leaped ashore before the guards could grab him. In the process, he'd wrenched his crossbow from one of the guards. As soon as he got onshore, he aimed his arrow towards his enemy, the despotic Gessler. It all happened before the guards could react.

Now, with William on the shore and armed, the guards turned to their leader to see if they could save his life. At once, they saw that he was gone, a dead man.

They turned their attention to William who by now had been joined by his son, Walter, and his followers, including Billy. The guards did not try any action; they waited for William to tell them what was next to come.

"Come Walter," William said to his son, "and Hans, and Billy, follow me." He said nothing to the two guards left in the boat; they would have to fend for themselves.

As quick as lightning, William, Walter, Billy, and Hans scrambled into the bushes and on into the woods. They quickly disappeared from sight.

The guards again turned their attention to the slumped-over Gessler. They tried to revive him, but he was dead, dead, dead—shot through the heart by the best marksman in Switzerland, who had now escaped them and was lost in the nearby forest.

"We've no prisoner," said one of the guards. "There's no one to take to our jail."

"Yes," said the other guard. "And, our leader is dead. Come, we'll carry him to the station." The jail was located about a half-mile away, right on the shore. The guards attached a rope to the boat and they moved it, holding the body of Gessler, along the shoreline until they reached the station.

Meanwhile, the four escapees paused in their flight. William needed to the next sequence of events.

"Billy," said William, "take Walter to my home. Tell his mother that I'll be there later tonight."

"Yes, I will," replied Billy, as he reached for Walter's small hand, to take the boy the few miles to his mother, at their home in the Swiss Alps.

It had been an eventful day. William had been arrested by Gessler that morning because he had refused to bow down to the hat that Gessler had placed on a pole in the town square. Soldiers had been placed near the pole, ready to arrest anyone who had not followed Gessler's dictate. Immediately upon passing the hat without bowing, William was arrested.

He was brought before Gessler. When the governor learned that this was William Tell, the well-known marksman in this country of Switzerland, he immediately set up a trial.

"I am generous," said Gessler, trying to appear magnanimous. "I'm willing to let you go free this time, as long as you can show me your skill with the crossbow and arrow."

"Aye," replied William, "I'm a modest man and not given to bragging, but I can show you that."

"Alright," said Gessler, teasingly, "I've been told that you have great skill, that you are the foremost marksman in all of Switzerland."

"No, not me," said William, modestly. "There are many better marksmen than I am."

"Well, we'll see how good you are," said Gessler, not willing to parry words with this simple mountain man. "We'll have you shoot an apple off your son's head. If you can do that, we will claim you to be the best marksman in Switzerland."

William was a little stunned and annoyed at this challenge. He knew he was good, an accurate marksman, but he was unhappy to have to put his son in peril. He developed a simple plan.

Just after Noon, he and his son, Walter, were brought to the village square. His son was placed in front of a large tree and an apple was balanced atop his head.

Nearby to William were his comrades, Hans and Billy. The guards recognized them as being patriots and that they were part of William's group. Billy and Hans stayed about ten feet away from William as he prepared for his ordeal.

William walked over to his son and spoke quietly to him and to assure him that all would be right.

"Don't worry, my boy," confided William, as he whispered to Walter, "I'll not miss. You are safe. Just close your eyes and everything will be all right. The important thing is that you must stand very still. When you hear me say "Ready" do not move, do not move even one muscle!"

Walter stood erect, the apple on his head. His father walked ten paces, as required by Gessler, turned and aimed his crossbow. He lowered the crossbow, wet his finger and held it up. He was checking windage, how much wind was blowing and from which direction. Hans and Billy stood nearby to support William but not to interfere with the action.

Again, William raised his crossbow. The crowd that had gathered held their breath. Some said a quiet prayer.

"Ready," he said, loud enough for Walter to hear. Walter stiffened and stood rigid.

Zing! The arrow flashed toward young Walter. It hit the apple right in the middle and the two halves flew in opposite directions. The arrow, quivering slightly, lodged itself in the tree trunk. William lowered his crossbow.

"That was well done," said Gessler, somewhat surprised that the apple had been hit with no harm to the boy. He had quietly hoped that William Tell would miss, maybe not hit his son, but would miss, and show himself to be not as good a marksman as had been claimed.

Young Walter ran to William and stood fast against his leg as his father gently stroked his son's blond hair. Gessler stood and was about to leave the viewing platform. One of the guards whispered something to him.

"Wait a minute," said Gessler, turning suddenly and staring at William. "You have another arrow in your quiver. Why did you have an extra arrow when you needed only one to split the apple?"

"My son is dear to me," replied William, honestly, as he proudly rose to his full height. "If I had harmed him, the second arrow would have been lodged in your heart!"

"That's treason!" shouted Gessler. "Arrest him. Guards, take that man into custody."

Four guards quickly pinned William's arms behind his back, his crossbow had fallen at his feet. They bound him tightly. Other guards bound Billy and Hans.

"We'll show you our might; we'll take you right to prison, right now!" said Gessler. "Johann, get the boat and let's be off." They were taking William Tell to the prison on the far side of the lake.

Gessler, two of the guards, William, along with young Walter, Hans, and Billy, stepped into the boat. The two guards began to row. The sky became dark. A storm, and a strong one at that, was about to crash upon them.

"Let's hurry," said Gessler. "We want to get across before the storm comes."

"Yes, sir," answered one of the guards. They doubled their efforts as they bent strongly to the oars, rowing as rapidly as they could.

But, they couldn't outrace the storm. When they were within a hundred yards of the distant shore, the storm broke. Thunder rolled and lightning flashed. The waves grew higher and white caps formed atop them. The oarsmen made no progress and the boat just heaved up and down.

"Untie him, unchain him" said Gessler to the guards. "He can do the rowing and get us there."

They untied William and seated him at the oars. William Tell's strong arms began to pull the boat towards the shore. However, it moved laterally. At one point Gessler thought that William was deliberately avoiding the intended landing point, the pier near the government station, where the prison was located.

"Keep a steady course there," commanded Gessler. This command fell on deaf ears. William knew what he was doing and, yes, he was deliberately rowing towards a spot on the shore that was about a mile away from the prison pier. There was nothing Gessler could do about it.

Within a short time the boat bottom crunched on the sand at the shoreline, the place that William had intended to reach.

Before the guards could scramble out of the boat, William pushed two of them aside, grabbed his crossbow and fitted an arrow to it. He jumped onto the shore, turned and shot Gessler through the heart. It happened so quickly, in only a few seconds.

The guards were trying to recover themselves and to attend to Gessler, who was slumped over.

Billy grabbed young Walter and he and Hans leaped from the boat and stood next to William.

"There's noting more to do here," said William, as they melted into the forest, "let's keep going."

They paused after a few minutes.

"Hans, you come with me," said William, "and Billy, you take Walter to my home."

William and Hans disappeared into the dense under-growth and on into the forest. Billy took young Walter to his home and delivered the message to Mrs. Tell. He ate the meal that she had just prepared and then told her he would go to the gathering place that he knew William was at.

Billy shook hands with Walter, put on his hat and left the house. He turned to wave at Walter and his mother, and then faded into the forest. He brushed aside a small branch and suddenly discovered it was Thalia's arm that he was trying to brush aside.

"Sweetheart," said Thalia. "You're awake. No need to push me away. I'm here to help you."

Billy slowly realized that he was lying on the couch in the doctor's office and Thalia had just touched his arm as he began to wave it.

"I was just pushing a branch out of the way," said Billy, still unclear about the branch and the sofa and Thalia, and waking up in the doctor's office.

"Did you get to see William Tell?" asked Thalia, eagerly.

"Oh, yes," said Billy, full of enthusiasm. "I was right there, standing next to William as he shot the apple off his son's head. Oh, it was some sight, I'll tell you!"

"And," he added, "I was in the boat, going across the stormy lake when they let William free to man the oars. His rowing ability got us across the lake and he jumped onto the shore and shot Gessler right through the heart! He killed that dastardly fellow right there—and I was in the center of all of that action. Oh, it was a real treat. I'm still worked up about it."

The doctor had been taking notes while Billy described his adventure. Thalia was happy that Billy was so excited about his participation. His pulse rate had jumped and his blood pressure had shot up. Now, all of that was coming down to normal level.

Billy, still a bit in a fog, sat on the sofa and breathed heavily, excited for several minutes after we woke up.

"That really was something!" was all he could say.

"You were present when the people of Switzerland were about to gain their independence," said Thalia. "That was a very big event at that time."

"It sure was," replied Billy. "That mountainous country would have been difficult to govern; those Swiss are a tough, industrious people, and they wouldn't have permitted any nation to rule them."

"Did you know that the opera composer, Rossini, composed an opera about William Tell?" asked Thalia.

"No, I didn't know that," replied Billy.

"Nor I," chimed in Dr. Dulcamara. "Have you ever heard that opera?"

"Not the full opera," responded Thalia. "But I have heard the overture. And, it is stirring! When you hear the overture, you can just imagine the gathering of the people to fight off Gessler and his minions."

"A William Tell opera! Let's put that down on our list of things to do," said Billy. "Now that I've been helping William Tell, I'd anxious to see and hear an opera about him."

"Bravo!" laughed Thalia.

Chapter 6

Patrick Henry of Virginia

"So," said Dr. Dulcamara, "you are all set for your next session?"

"Yes," said Billy Costello, "Thalia and I have been talking about one of our earliest national heroes and I want to be present when he speaks."

"And his name is?" queried the doctor.

"Patrick Henry!" exclaimed Billy, with enthusiasm.

"You see, doctor," said Thalia, "Billy and I both admire many of our earlier patriots and Patrick Henry was a strong advocate of liberty for these colonies. Before our War for Independence, which we call the Revolutionary War, this man, Patrick Henry, stood up forcefully against the King of England and all that he represented, especially the tyrannical governance of that king."

"Of course," said the doctor, "like most Europeans, I'm aware of your unique struggle against England seventy or eighty years ago, but I'm not informed as to the details of much of what happened."

"Well," said Thalia, "our revolution was unique. We believed in the common man—that was unique. We felt that our leaders had not been ordained by God, even though the established church said so. In fact, we knew that the established religion in any country was hand-in-hand with the government. That stifled democracy."

"Patrick Henry," she went on, "was a Virginia lawyer and legislator. He was eloquent in calling for the doctrine of natural rights, the political theory that man is born with certain inalienable rights. And, in every speech he would try to bring up that subject—saying that the rights of the common man were sacred and inviolate. He said so in the Virginia legislature and on every occasion that he could."

"Doctor," said Billy, "back during our revolution there was great danger to anyone who spoke out against the British authority. It was quickly labeled as treason. And being convicted of treason would land you in jail for years and perhaps get your head cut off. It was truly dangerous to speak out against King George the Third of England during that time."

"But," added Thalia, "Patrick Henry was brave. He seemed to care not a whit whether he was accused of treason or disloyalty to the king. He was mainly interested in talking about individual rights—the rights of the subjects being governed. That made him very unusual."

"It was true of many prominent men," said Billy. "Even the Father of our Country, George Washington, was in constant danger because he was the leader of the troops that were fighting the redcoats of King George. If the English had won the war, Washington, Jefferson, John Adams, Samuel Adams, and many, many others would have been executed— hung or guillotined or whatever."

"I didn't know all of that," said Dr. Dulcamara. "As you can imagine, we in Europe received only scant information about your revolution. Of course, I knew you had won and that the British had lost, but many of the details, like the ones that you've just told me, were unknown to me."

"Those were brave men back then," said Billy, admiringly.

"Yes, they were," said the doctor. "In many historical times, there are very brave men, and some women, who have lost their lives because they opposed the government and, in some times, they've been against the established church."

"That's what this country is trying to do," said Billy. "We're trying to establish a government that respects the individual, the rights of the citizens. And, doesn't allow any particular religion to dictate the rules whereby we live. It's all right for the religion to tell their members what to do, but that's as far as it goes. Don't tell the rest of the citizens how to live and don't demand that they obey the rules of any particular religion."

"But," laughed Billy, "we're getting too far afield. We've suddenly gotten into a good discussion, but you have a test to run and I'm the willing patient, ready to undergo the treatment that you have arranged."

"Yes, yes," laughed the doctor, "it's so easy to get into a discussion where religion and politics are concerned. You're right, it's time to get our next experiment underway."

Billy sat on the couch and Thalia arranged the large cushions for him to relax against. Dr. Dulcamara picked up his notepad and pulled a chair close to Billy.

"Now, Billy," he said, "I want you to look fixedly at that small plant in the pot on the stand right over there. Keep looking at it and try not to blink for a short while until I tell you."

Billy stared at the small plant. He didn't blink. About twenty seconds passed when the doctors quietly said: "Billy, blink your eyes and go to sleep."

Immediately, Billy's head fell off towards his right shoulder and he slumped against the cushions. He was unconscious, in dreamland.

Billy heard a voice calling to him. "Billy, we need you over here." He turned to see who it was.

Billy was in Richmond, Virginia, and the man calling to him was on the steps of St. John's Church.

Billy walked up the steps and over towards his friends.

"Billy," said Al Kemp, "we're about to go in to hear Mr. Henry give his speech. You wanted to come with us, so here we are. Let's get to our places."

Al, Bob Dorn, and Sam Smith greeted Billy as he came up the steps. They went into the church and sat near the front, so they could hear well.

"Mr. Henry is a real firebrand," said Al. "He's been known to defy any authority."

"Yes, that's true," added Bob Dorn, "but what he says is truthful and it fits the people. He's well known for speaking for the people, the common man, for us guys."

"I really don't know a lot about him," said Billy. "Like everybody else, I know his name and that he's a famous orator, but that's about it. Tell me more, what's his background?"

"He's a real live Virginian," responded Al, "and a patriot, to boot. His father was a justice of the County Court. He tried farming and store-keeping but he was too ambitious for those fields, so he studied law and became a lawyer."

"Yeah," added Bob, "he was some trial lawyer. He won a great case by invoking individual rights. And, from that time on he's been known as a man who supports the rights of the individual. He hates any government that acts tyrannically."

"Some time ago, I think it was in 1765, in the Virginia legislature where he'd been elected to," said Sam. "That's when he really spoke out, practically spitting in the face of King George himself!"

"What he said," added Sam, "and I remember it well because we had to learn it word for word in lawyer's school, was, during a speech in the capitol at Williamsburg, (and it was in 1765) he said: '*Caesar had his Brutus, Charles the First his Cromwell, and George the Third...*' but he was interrupted by some of the other members shouting **Treason!**

Treason! He paused for a moment and then continued: *'and George the Third may profit by their example. If this be treason, make the most of it!'* Boy, was he defiant."

"Now, you've got to stop and think," said Bob. "When Patrick Henry made that speech in 1765, most of the politicians in Virginia were loyal to King George. Anything that anyone said, that was in opposition to the King, was considered treason."

"And," added Al, "that was what Mr. Henry was speaking against—tyranny. King George had imposed taxes and repressive measures on us people. He had taken away some of our liberties, liberties that the people in England had but that we were denied. We were being treated like second-class citizens. Mr. Henry was speaking about individual liberties and he was adamant about that. He said that the King was wrong and should change the way we were being governed."

"Of course," he added, "when he said that the king was wrong, well, it amounted to treason in the minds of those who were loyal to the king. But Patrick Henry felt his first loyalty was to the people, to the individuals, and he wanted to see those rights restored to the people, not taken away from them."

"Well," said Billy, "that was 1765, ten years ago. There's been a lot happened since. Here it is, the 23rd of March 1775, so what do we expect to hear from Patrick Henry today?"

"I'm not sure," replied Al, "but I'll bet it has to do with individual rights, maybe something to do with liberty or that sort of thing."

"There's been a lot going on," Bob reminded them. "Those guys up in New England are defying everything that the King is throwing against them. Didn't you guys hear about that Tea Party? They threw the tea off the ship right into the harbor, ruined it all."

"Well, they did that to protest the tax on tea," said Sam. "My uncle was one of those who were dressed as Indians who threw off that tea."

"And, do you know why?" asked Al. "Because we were taxed on tea but the people in Old England were not taxed on tea. It was unfair."

"Well," responded Bob, "I'm not sure that the English people were not taxed, it was just that we were. It seemed that King George wanted to tax a lot of things—documents, title papers, lots of dinky little things, and it was annoying. It seemed like he was just chipping at the bone, trying to take a little here and take a little there. That's been the main problem."

"Hey," cautioned Al, "they're about to be introduced."

"Ladies and Gentlemen," said the man who was to introduce the panel of speakers, all representatives of the Virginia Convention. "To my right, at the table, is the committee on Current Events. They will now address you." Among those members was Patrick Henry.

There was polite applause as the first committee member rose to speak. After his short speech, came another short talk by a second member. Now it was Patrick Henry's turn to speak.

When he rose to speak, he looked out over the crowd. The audience applauded. Everyone was very much in favor of this man. For the past ten years, he had been an influential leader in the radical opposition to the British government and the audience knew that. They hoped to hear a speech advocating more strenuous opposition.

"My friends," he began, "our chains are getting tighter. It pains me to stand here and tell you that there is no longer any room for hope. We must arm. Now, hear me loud and clear: We must arm. If we wish to be free, **we must fight!** Gentlemen may cry **Peace, Peace**, but there is no **Peace.** The war has actually begun! Let me repeat that: *the war has actually begun!*'" He thumped his fist into his other hand.

"Why stand we here idle? Our brethren to the North are armed and ready for the fight. What is it that gentlemen wish for? What is it that they would have?"

"Is life so dear and peace so sweet," he thundered, "that it can be purchased at the price of chains and slavery!" He paused and then said: "Forbid it, Almighty God!"

Patrick Henry speaks "Give me liberty or...,"

Here he again paused and, with a stern and fixed stare, he looked out over the audience that was stunned by his words, and now awaited his next thunderbolt. He stepped forward, right to the front edge of the dais level on which he stood and, spreading his arms outward, said:

"I know not what course others may take, but as for me, give me liberty or give me death!"

The audience sat stunned for a moment. The other speakers stared in awe at this slender man, standing there saying that liberty was far more valuable to him that chains or death.

Suddenly, the audience exploded into cheers and applause. There were shouts and many listeners turned to pat their neighbors on the back. Agreement with Patrick Henry was universal. He had charged up the audience with his patriot fervor.

."Boy," said Al, "that was some speech. I'm ready to go off and enlist, right now. I'm with Patrick Henry. What a speaker!"

"He's a spell-binder, that's for sure," said Bob. "And, he's right. We've got to fight. The Brits have misused us for years and years now. It won't get any better, it'll only get worse. We've got to fight!"

Patrick Henry's speech ended the session. Nothing of any importance could follow that speech. The audience and speakers milled around, most of them clustered near Patrick Henry. He spoke to many of them.

Billy was stunned. He sat in his seat for some minutes, listening to the words of his friends and picking up snatches of conversation from others.

"Al," said Billy to his friend, "that was the most moving speech I've ever heard. It appears that the war is underway and that we are on a course to fight for our freedom."

"Yes," answered Al. "It's not only going to happen, it is happening. We don't see it much here in Richmond, but they've had some skirmishes up there near Boston. It's like a powder keg there, ready to blow up any day now."

Billy and his friends slowly went outside the church and sat on the top level of the steps. They watched the people come out. Everyone was excited, everyone was caught up in the emotional feelings of the moment.

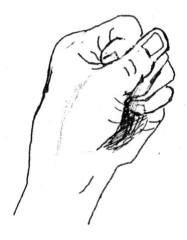

"This tyranny has been going on for a long time," said Al, to no one in particular, but his friends listened to him. "It has just finally come to this—that the only way we'll get out from under this tyrannical rule is to gain our independence. We must become an independent nation."

"I agree," said Bob. "For years and years, practically since the Pilgrims landed in 1620, we've been treated like servants by the English rulers. There has to be a stop to that at some time, and now appears to be the time."

"It's coming, it's coming," said Sam, a little ruefully. "I hate to see war come. I was in several fights in the Caribbean area and, believe me, they are no fun. People get killed! People get hurt, arms are torn off and legs are lost. I hate to see it come, but if there's no alternative, then it must take place. God help us all!"

The four of them sat quietly, each with his own thoughts. Just then Patrick Henry came out of the church, accompanied by a large group of people.

"I'm going over there to hear what he's saying," said Al, as he quickly rose. "Me, too," added Bob and Sam, together. They left Billy where he was sitting.

Billy sat alone for a few minutes, thinking about what he'd just heard—the speech of a lifetime. His mind was trying to picture what was going to happen: battles, flags waving, defeats, victories, shells exploding, and so on. Suddenly, he realized that he was awakening in the doctor's office.

There's Billy!" exclaimed Dr. Dulcamara, as he saw Billy's eyes flutter. "He's back with us."

"Honey," said Thalia, as she gently rubbed her husband's shoulders, "you're back home. Did you have an eventful trip? Did you get to see Patrick Henry?"

"Oh, yes," said Billy, excitedly. "I was right there when he said *Give me Liberty or Give me Death!* What a grand moment for our country's history and for me! It was all that I could have imagined."

"Isn't that wonderful, doctor," said Thalia to Dr. Dulcamara, "Billy actually was in the same room as Patrick Henry when that famous speech was given! What an historic event, what a wonderful experience." Thalia was just as enthusiastic as Billy as he began to talk about his experience.

"It was a truly stirring speech," said Billy. "Anyone who was there and heard it must have been moved. Mind you, some who heard it, the loyalists, were moved in the other, unpatriotic direction. But, I'm talking about the true Americans, those who were crying out for freedom from the mother country."

"When they stormed out of that hall that day," he added, "everyone of them was ready to go home and clean up their muskets. They were ready to fight for independence!"

The doctor asked a few more questions of Billy, and then Thalia took over. "We're going to have dinner out tonight. We're going to the restaurant. You've got me too excited to cook, plus I want to hear more and more about Patrick Henry."

"Well, my dear," answered Billy. "It will be my treat. Buying dinner for you, my darling, is a lot easier than fighting for independence back in 1775. I'm glad that our side won. We are the benefactors, now."

"Amen," said Thalia, as she handed him his coat and they prepared to leave Dr. Dulcamara.

Chapter 7

Betsy Ross

"As you know, Billy," said his wife, Thalia, "our flag is very important to us. And, we had several flags before it was decided that the one we now have, would be **the one**."

"Yes, my dear," replied her husband, with deep-seated feeling, "there's nothing that stirs me more and gives me chills more, than to see our flag floating along in a parade. I always salute it when it goes by."

"You said that there was once a snake flag," he queried.

"Oh, yes," replied Thalia. "I think that Ben Franklin devised that one. It had a snake, cut into pieces with each piece representing one of the thirteen states. And, it had a message—that the states must hang together or they'd all hang separately."

"That was a pretty witty saying," said Billy. "In that, if the rebellion did not result in the colonies winning the war, then the most prominent members would 'hang separately'."

"Yes, that was a chilling statement," added Thalia. "In those early days of our revolution, there was real and constant danger to those men—George Washington, John Adams, Benjamin Franklin, Thomas Jefferson, and many others. If we'd lost, they would have been killed, executed—almost certainly by being hung!"

"But," replied Billy, "we came out on top, we won. So, actually no important people, those trying to form a government here in America, or those leading England against us, were hung or lost their heads."

"That was a very interesting result of our American Revolution," added Thalia. "In most countries, revolutions result in leaders dying, losing their heads, being guillotined, or exiled, or whatever. In the case of our new country, after the peace treaty was signed, no one died because he was unlucky enough to be on the wrong side. The winners, the conspirators, did not seek out the losers and kill them. Our new leaders, the winners, simply got on with establishing our country. That was enough of a difficult task, and it took most of their time."

"Well, here we are at the doctor's office," said Billy, "ready to make our next trip back in history."

"Hello, Dr. Dulcamara," said Billy, as he and Thalia, entered the office.

"Hello to my favorite couple, the Costellos!" replied the doctor, full of enthusiasm and happy to see his friends again. "Come in, come in."

It was a Wednesday early afternoon in the middle of June 1856. Billy and Thalia were helping the doctor in his research of the new wonders of hypnotism. The doctor was investigating the uses of hypnotism that might help his medical practice.

"Do you have a subject that you wish to visit?" asked the doctor.

"Yes," said Billy, acting nonchalantly. "I'm going to try to go back about eighty years to the founding of our country, back to the time when the first flag was designed and produced."

"What a wonderful subject!" exclaimed Dr. Dulcamara. "I am constantly amazed at you and your wife. You choose such interesting historical people and events."

"Well," said Billy, as he gave his wife a friendly squeeze, "you must credit my wife, Thalia. She is a storehouse of knowledge and a walking encyclopedia. She knows everything about everything!"

"Ha, Ha!" laughed Thalia. "Don't be fooled. There is much that I do not know. But, when I do know about some historical event, I can usually get Billy prepared for the upcoming session. Billy is an eager learner and he's willing to take on any challenge."

The doctor reached over and took Thalia's hand. Looking at both of them, he said: "What a lovely couple you are. You are so fit for each other, so agreeable. It is so nice for me to see such a well-knit couple. I wish there would be more like you two in our community or in any community."

Billy and Thalia looked at each other and smiled. They knew they were a good fit and they were pleased that the doctor noticed it, too. They tried to get along, they truly tried to help each other. It wasn't just words, it was action—they knew how to make the other person happy.

"Well, let's get started," said the doctor, as he began to prepare for this session.

Billy, who had done this before, took a seat on the couch and Thalia propped two large pillows behind him. The doctor took a chair near Billy's head and Thalia sat in a chair just behind Billy.

"Now, Billy," said Dr. Dulcamara, "just hold this red piece of cloth in your two hands. I am laying two more small cloths on top, one is white and one is blue. Now I want you to pull these cloths up and lay them over your eyes."

All this was said in a low monotone. The doctor continued:

"Now, Billy imagine that you are looking into and through these three pieces of colored cloth. Keep trying to look into and through them. Keep trying. Keep trying."

His voice trailed off until Billy could hear it no more and suddenly he found himself walking with three gentlemen on a street, actually a narrow alley, in colonial Philadelphia.

The three gentlemen, along with Billy and several other aides, approached the front door of the tailor's shop located on a narrow street between Philadelphia's City Hall and the Delaware River. It was the middle of May 1776. Of the three, one man was much taller than the others. The tall man opened the front door to the shop.

Betsy Ross meets the Flag Committee

"Ah, there you are, Mrs. Ross, Betsy Ross!"—a friendly greeting indeed from the tall gentleman in military uniform. Obviously, the tall man and Mrs. Ross knew each other.

"Yes, Sir," replied the lady, as she curtsied slightly. She wanted to show the utmost respect to her visitors. "I'm Betsy. My mother named me Elizabeth, but I've been called Betsy since I was a little girl," she smiled.

"Well, we've come here to ask if you could perform a service for your country," the tall man continued. "You may remember me because my wife, Martha, has asked you to do some of your expert tailoring for us."

"Oh, yes, General Washington," admiringly replied Betsy, "I'd know you anywhere. And your wife and I have met on several occasions." Betsy was a step lower in class than Martha Washington, although that wasn't a real reason to feel inferior, here in the newly-forming republic. But, she knew her place and was happy with it.

"These are my associates," he gently waved to the two men who accompanied him, who each took a step forward. "Mr. Robert Morris and Colonel George Ross, the uncle of your late husband. We want to talk to you about helping us in a project that we have in mind."

Billy and the other aides stayed one step behind, each one directly behind his master.

As each man was introduced, Betsy made a modest curtsey. The men bowed in turn and her uncle, George, reached over to touch her gently on the shoulder.

"Please have a seat," said Betsy, as she showed them to a settee and some chairs. When they were seated, Billy stood directly behind General Washington, ready to help at any request.

"Betsy," said Washington, "here in a nutshell is what we want. **We need a national flag, a national flag for our country**. As you and everyone knows, we're fighting for independence from Great Britain and we are determined that *we will not use the British flag as our country's flag!"*—he said this with very strong emphasis, but without rancor—"We need a flag of our own! An ensign that speaks of us and our new country."

"I have with me a pattern," he continued, more moderately, "and we need your talents as a seamstress or tailor to make the stars in the field of the flag. We cannot decide if we should have a star with six-points or five-points. Can you make such a star and sew it into the flag?"

"Sir," said Betsy, with a self-assured, lilting laugh, "I've been sewing since I was a tiny child. I was taught well and carefully in my Quaker school. I can make a star, any type that you want and it will be sewn into any place on the flag that you ask for. Here, let me show you."

Betsy took a small piece of cloth. She folded it several ways and reached for her large scissors. After a few quick snips, she unfolded the finished item and there it was—a five-pointed star!

"My goodness," exclaimed George Washington, admiringly, "that was miraculous! You are very clever and have great ability. You are a very gifted woman." He picked up the star and held it for his colleagues to see. They passed it around, each person examining it closely.

Betsy had grown up as a Quaker and had attended school where she learned reading and writing and sewing. It was a Quaker essential that all children should be productive and useful. However, she had fallen in love with John Ross, an Episcopalian. They had eloped to New Jersey, just across the river from Philadelphia, and married. When they came back to Philadelphia, as was the custom, her Quaker church "read her out", that is, they shunned her and did not recognize her any more. She would receive no assistance from her church members.

Nevertheless, being young and in love, she and John felt that they could deal with any adversity. They opened an upholstery-and-sewing shop and eventually John joined the Colonial Army to help with family income. Unfortunately, in mid-January 1776, John was mortally wounded and died.

Now, as a young widow, her Quaker church members brought her back into the fold. They reconnected and welcomed her. Her Quaker friends gave her much help and she did her best to earn an adequate income. She would wed again in June 1977, a year after the visit from the flag committee.

Meanwhile, the first flag needed to be born and this fine Philadelphia seamstress, Betsy Ross, was the one to act as the birthing partner.

"Billy," Washington said as he turned to the young man standing behind him, "hand me the plan layout for the flag, the one that you're carrying."

"Here it is, Sir," said Billy, as he took the rolled-up parchment from his coat pocket and handed it to the General.

"Now, Mrs. Ross, let me show you what we have in mind," Washington said to Betsy. He stood up and laid out the parchment on a table.

He opened up the sketch so that Betsy could see the design. George Ross and Robert Morris stood beside Washington as they leaned over the table. Billy Costello stood next to Washington's left side.

"As you can see, Betsy," said Washington, (he alternately called her Betsy and Mrs. Ross), "what we want is stripes, alternately red and white, seven red and six white, with a blue field in the upper left corner. In the blue field we want thirteen stars, representing our thirteen states."

"I see your plan," said Mrs. Ross, as she looked over the design, "and it seems to me to be a rather simple job. By that I mean, it is not a complex undertaking. I do not see any difficult complications. It will take time and materials, of course, but that is true of any design. My shop can readily accommodate your requests. I can have a sample ready for you by the end of next week."

"Fine," said Washington. "We will, of course, pay you for your services and we will either supply the cloth or we will reimburse you if you buy the cloth. We will need at least six flags made very soon; they will be reviewed by the Congress and, if they are approved, we will then need many more manufactured, either by you or under your direction."

"I'll be happy to have the business," replied Betsy, with a wide smile. She knew that this could be a very successful contract. "I can change anything you request and I can make some flags here in my shop. If a great many flags are needed, I can act as a supervisor at some other manufacturing plant. I can arrange all of these things."

"That's fine," said Washington, with a smile. "I'm very happy that we have such an excellent artisan as you. Now here is what we will need in the next week or so."

"Billy, please take notes of this," said Washington to his aide, Billy, who immediately whipped out his notepad and began to write.

First, he told Betsy that the prototype that she would make would be picked up from her next Friday. He then outlined the size and proportions of the next six flags that Betsy would produce, following the pattern that they had just discussed. She named her price and when the flags would be ready. Billy recorded all of the information.

"That should take care of everything," said Washington, as he arose to leave. "When the first flag, the prototype, is ready for delivery, let me know and I will send some one to pick it up. From the account of your timetable, that appears to be next Friday."

"After that, Congress must confer and approve," he added. "I'm sure that they will approve. There will be a lapse of a week or two, then we should return with modifications or an order for more flags. I suspect that any modifications will be minor, indeed."

"I will be most happy to oblige," said Betsy, as she curtsied. The men all smiled and took their leave.

Betsy turned to her one helper and said: "Saints be praised, we have enough work to keep us busy for the next two or three weeks, and more! Now, there should be no delay—let's start in right this very moment!"

As the men walked out the door and away from the shop, Billy handed the notes to General Washington. He took them, placing them in his large pocket and nodded "Thanks" to Billy. Billy felt extremely proud to be walking along with General Washington and the other men.

They walked a short distance and came to a corner. The three men went East as Billy went North. The scene slowly faded from his view. He opened his eyes to find himself on Doctor Dulcamara's couch. Thalia was smiling at him.

"You're back!" she shouted. "Did you see our first flag? Was General Washington there?" The questions tumbled out of her.

"Yes, yes, and yes!" said Billy, as he was trying to wipe away the cobwebs from his mind. He slowly sat up on the couch. Dr. Dulcamara, notebook in hand, was smiling broadly, pleased with the session.

"You were gone for twenty-eight minutes," he said to Billy, "and you were very quiet. Only once did you move your hands as if you were reaching into your pocket for something, trying to get whatever it was out of your pocket."

"Oh, I know what it was," laughed Billy. "It was the parchment with the drawings for the flag. General Washington had asked me for the drawings that I was carrying in my pocket and I retrieved them and handed them to him."

"Then, it was a real, real-life experience for you?" asked the doctor. "You felt like you were actually there?"

"Oh yes!" exclaimed Billy. "I *was* there. It was so real. If I had a pencil and could draw, I'd draw a face for everyone that was in the room where we discussed the new flag, in Betsy Ross' house."

"What did Betsy Ross look like?" asked Thalia.

"She was short, not tall, a little shorter than you are," replied Billy, "and she had on a long apron. Her hair was brown and it was curly or wavy. She had very small hands. And, she wore no noticeable jewelry. But, her smile! What a warm, endearing smile! When she smiled at any of the men in the committee, they agreed immediately with her. That smile was a winner, a true winner."

The doctor asked Billy a few more questions. Soon, Billy and Thalia left his office, to return home. It had been an ennobling experience for Billy and he felt like Betsy Ross was still smiling on him.

Chapter 8

Nathan Hale

"So, you think that Nathan Hale was a great hero?" asked Billy of his wife, Thalia, as they were nearing the medical office of Dr. Dulcamara.

Dr. Dulcamara, a relatively young doctor from Europe, who had come to town recently, was conducting experiments in hypnotism. Billy and Thalia were his most important patients. They were willing to undergo hypnosis for the doctor's study and experimentation. They had devised a method of trying to dream about a historical person while they were asleep. So far, it had worked well and they had been present, or so they dreamed, at several important historical events.

"Yes," she replied. "Every time I think of Nathan Hale, that tender-aged twenty-one year old, I'm ready to cry. He was far too young to die. He was far too brave to die. See that," she said as she wiped away a tear, "I'm already getting teary-eyed. I just can't help it!"

"My goodness," exclaimed Billy, as he stopped to momentarily pause in their walk. He looked closely at his wife, "you are caught up in that young man's tragedy."

"I'm sorry," she said, "I just can't help it. I feel like he was my younger brother. To have him snatched away from me and us, just gives me goose pimples. I can't help it."

"You may not know it," she continued, "but he was born into a very good family. He was a bright young man. He began studying at Yale College when he was just thirteen. He was a good debater in college and he graduated, with first-class honors mind you, when he was just eighteen."

"What did he do when he graduated from Yale?" asked Billy.

"He became a teacher, a well-liked teacher," said Thalia. "But as soon as the Revolutionary War began in 1775, he was, like so many young men, anxious to join the patriots who wanted to sever relations with England. He joined the militia and was made a lieutenant. He soon moved over to the Continental Army and was made a Captain."

"I want to hear some more about Nathan Hale, but we're here, at the doctor's office," said Billy. "You've done an excellent job, as usual, because you've given me the subject for the day. I will try to be present at Nathan Hale's hanging."

"Well, there's the story of his hanging," said Thalia, sadly. "That's what bothers me the most."

"Yes, darling," replied Billy. "Before the doctor gets ready to put me to sleep, I want to know about that hanging."

They opened the door to the office and greeted the young doctor. He was expecting them and had prepared for the session that they would take part in. He was nearly ready for his next experiment, which was putting Billy to sleep by way of hypnotism. While Billy was asleep, the doctor would closely observe his behavior, studying everything that Billy would do while he was unconscious. Additionally, he was interested in any dreams that Billy might have while he was asleep.

"You've chosen a date in time or a subject?" asked Dr. Dulcamara. "Is it some historical event or some special person who lived long ago?"

"Yes," answered Billy. "This time it is Nathan Hale."

"Nathan Hale?" questioned the doctor. "I've never heard of him, as far as I can remember."

"Well, he is a great hero to us Americans," smiled Billy. "He was a very young man, barely twenty years old, and, during our Revolutionary War, he gave up his life for the new country that was forming, the country that would become the United States."

"Yes," added Thalia, "it is a very, very sad story. He was a very bright young man. He was only thirteen years old when he began to attend Yale College in New Haven, in the New England State of Connecticut, back on our Eastern Coast. I can hardly talk about it without crying."

"Well," said the doctor, "I'm really sorry that I've not heard about this young man, this hero. I hope that Billy will connect with that time in the past, and will be able to tell us more when he re-awakens."

"Are you ready, Billy" asked Dr. Dulcamara.

"Yes, sir," answered Billy. "I'm rarin' to go. I've done this a few times, now, and I feel like it is getting to be a routine. I guess the more I do it, the easier it will become."

"That's the way it should work," answered the doctor. "But you are an unusual person. You are strong and you want to do your part to participate. Some people, I'm sure, would be apprehensive every time that they would be involved."

"Oh, it's kinda enjoyable," said Billy, enthusiastically. "I'm happy to be a part of your experiments. I trust you and, so far, I've had no ill effects from previous experiments, so I'm always ready for the next one."

"You can't imagine how much your statements mean to me," said the doctor. "Of course, I'm a very, very careful man and I will do you no harm. I'm glad that you do not feel ill at ease while we're doing these experiments."

"Nope. There's no problem here," said Billy, nonchalantly. "You're giving me the opportunity to connect with past historical events and people. That's a rare opportunity for anyone. I'm happy to be part of it."

"Thank you, thank you," said the doctor, graciously. "Just give me about three or four minutes and I'll be ready."

"Good," said Thalia to Billy. "Let me tell you some more about Nathan Hale."

"Good idea," replied Billy. "I'll take all the information that I can get."

"It was early in the Fall of 1776," said Thalia, "during the Battle of Long Island. He volunteered to go behind enemy lines and report on the British troop movements and where the gun emplacements were, as well as any other information that he could discover."

"While he was behind the enemy lines," she said, "the area around Wall Street, on the lower tip of Manhattan, fell to the British forces and Washington's troops retreated further north on the island, to near Harlem Heights."

"Suddenly, a large fire broke out in lower Manhattan," she continued, "and it burned over a lot of the area. The British believed that American patriots had set the fire and they rounded up about 200 citizens, including Nathan Hale. He wore a disguise as an ordinary local citizen but one of the British officers recognized him."

"The officer set a trap," she went on, "having some one pretend to be a patriot who agreed to meet Nathan and when that occurred, he was taken into custody. Evidence was found on him indicating that he was a spy."

"According to the warfare standards of the time," she said, "spies were hanged as illegal combatants, so he was hanged as a spy."

"I'm ready now," said the doctor as he approached Billy.

"I am, too," answered Billy. "Let's get it on!"

Billy sat on the sofa, reclining against some very large cushions. He had removed his boots.

"Now, Billy," said Dr. Dulcamara, "I want you to look at the wallpaper on the wall directly across the room. Start at the top and notice the design and follow it closely as you slowly gaze down the wall. Keep looking and moving slowly," he said, very quietly, as Billy stared at the opposite wall. Suddenly, Billy relaxed and lay back on the pillows. He was asleep, out of touch. Deeply asleep.

"Hey, Henry," asked Billy, "where is everyone going?"

"They're hanging some guy, not far from here," answered Henry, a storekeeper who had a shop in mid-Manhattan. "Come along and you'll see the real thing for yourself."

"Who is it?" asked Billy. "Who's being hanged?"

"I'm not sure," answered Henry, soberly. Then he pulled Billy close to him and whispered: "I think that it's one of our guys." As he said that, he looked furtively about to see if anyone heard him.

"You mean, it's one of our soldiers?" asked Billy, using the same low tones, and looking about as he said that.

"Yes, that's what I heard," replied Henry. "Apparently, one of our guys was spying on the British (and who isn't?)," he said, quietly. "If they wanted to, they could hang nearly all of us; truthfully, we're all in this together."

"Yes," responded Billy, "except for those Loyalists. They're not spies. They want the British to win. They don't want us to be independent. Why is that, Henry?"

"It's a matter of how your bread is buttered, I think," replied Henry. "Those who want to keep British rule are prosperous under that rule. But they are the few. The many, most of us, are not prosperous under that rule. The British rules are too onerous; they treat us like second-class or third-class citizens. We're much, much lower than the citizens of England, our home country, where most of us came from."

"Why should we be treated so poorly?" he asked, seeming to grow more and more angry. "We're no better than slaves, really." As he spoke he kept looking about to see who might hear his words. They continued to walk towards a grassy area where a gibbet, a gallows stand, had been erected.

Young Nathan Hale about to be hanged

"There it is," exclaimed Henry, as they neared the execution site. "This is a park area, sometimes called Artillery Park. As we've been walking along Post Road, that's where they've marched the victim. They were a little ahead of us. See, they're about to do the job now."

Billy looked at the wooden platform where several soldiers stood. A young man, his hands tied behind his back, was ascending the steps, helped by soldiers on either side of him. The young man reached the platform and stood straight and tall.

An officer said to him: "Nathan Hale, do you have any last words before you die?"

"Yes, Sir" answered the young man, politely and in a civil manner, "I regret that I have only one life to give to my country!"

The British officer, a Captain, staggered back a step or two. The noble statement struck him. He was in his mid-forties and was old enough to be the father of this young man that was about to lose his life.

The Captain turned to his assistant. "Here, Joseph," he said, "you finish up. I'll wait on you below." Somehow, the Captain could not go through with the execution and was turning it over to his assistant. The Captain slowly climbed down the stairs to wait.

"Ready, men" said the executioner to the soldiers who stood next to Nathan Hale. A noose was fastened around his neck. The two soldiers stepped aside. The officer nodded and the trapdoor below Nathan's feet fell away and he fell through, hanging there, dead. Nathan Hale was now dead but he was alive in the hearts of every patriot in the young country called America.

"Oh, that's very sad," said Billy, as he turned away, not willing to see the swaying body of the young man, gently swaying at the end of the rope. "He was far, far too young to die. Death is so final. Now he has no chance for the future. He may have become a schoolmaster, maybe a college professor, maybe a political leader. It's just too, too sad to see someone so young, lose his life—and at the hands of others, in such a meaningless manner. I almost feel like throwing up."

"True," said Henry, as he too looked away from the swaying body. "War is terrible. I wish we could have accomplished this independence without any bloodshed. I hate to see the young die."

"Kill the old!" he exclaimed, barely aloud. "They've seen life. They've had their chances to do well, to do good. It doesn't seem right to take the life of a young man. What was this fellow, about twenty-one, I think?"

Billy and Henry walked back along the Post Road towards Henry's shop. They said very little as they walked, but they were both sad.

Once, Billy said: "I'll never forget those words. *I regret that I have only one life to give to my country!*"

Henry nodded his agreement and said: "He was a fine young man, a brave young man. And, he will be remembered!"

Quietly, he leaned towards Billy and whispered: "Damn the British! Damn them! I'll never forget this. Those rotten devils have turned me, and I'm sure thousands of others, against them. They'll lose! And, when they lose, I'll rejoice, but I'll always remember this young man!"

They walked a little further and Henry said: "I must turn here to go to my store. Good Day to you."

"Yes, Sir," replied Billy, "and Good Day to you."

Henry turned right and Billy continued on. Suddenly, he felt a stone in his boot. He sat on the ground and removed his boot. As he did so, he thought his other boot had a pebble in it and he removed it, too.

As he was beginning to put his boot back on his foot, he realized that he was on the sofa, in Dr. Dulcamara's office, and the doctor and Thalia were trying to help him put his boots back on.

"Oh," Billy exclaimed, "I never want to go through that again."

"Were you with Nathan Hale?" eagerly asked Thalia.

"Yes, yes," said Billy, resignedly. "And, it was very, very sad. It was 'way too sad. I admit that I'm glad I was there, but that's enough of hangings for me, especially the hanging of young people. I wouldn't want to witness another one."

"I think that you're getting the same feeling that I have about Nathan Hale," said Thalia. "It's just a terribly sad story. You can see why it brings me to tears."

"Oh, yes," said Billy. "He was far too young. He was such a promising young man. He would have been a fine person in our new country, an asset to help build the new republic. Yes, my dear, I now better understand your feelings about him."

"Doctor," said Billy, "I'll give you all of the details that you want about my trip involving Nathan Hale, but the sooner I put that out of my mind, the better I'm going to feel. It was just too, too sad for me to dwell on."

"I have made a lot of observations," said the doctor, "and I won't need any more about this particular experiment. You did a fine job and when you're rested, you're free to go."

"Thank you, doctor," said Billy. "I'm pretty well rested now and if you're ready, dear," he turned to Thalia, "let's get along home so that I can wash this event out of my mind."

"Here's your hat, dear," said Thalia. "I'm all set to go."

"Doctor," said Billy to the physician, "when you're ready for the next experiment, just let us know."

"It will probably be late next week, about Thursday," said the doctor. "I'll tell you when. And, thanks again for helping me today."

Chapter 9

The Death of Socrates

"Why would I be interested in that guy?" asked Billy of his wife, Thalia, as they walked toward Dr. Dulcamara's office. They were on the way to participate in another experiment of the doctor's, involving the new process of hypnosis. The doctor was attempting to understand hypnosis so that he could use it in treating his patients.

"Everybody should be interested in Socrates!" insisted Thalia. "He was one of the most important figures in ancient Greece."

"Well," answered Billy. "That was Greece, two thousand years ago and this is California, today! Where is the connection?"

"The connection is directly with democracy!" insisted Thalia. "Socrates was, in some ways, a mischief-maker. In other ways he was a supporter of the right. More often, he tried to have others view all sides of a discussion."

"Just imagine that you have come up with a solution to some problem here in the city," said Thalia. "You're convinced that you have the answer and you're anxious to get the problem solved your way."

"But," she went on, "have you tried to look at the opposite side of your solution, tried to see that your solution may not be effective, may even cause more problems?"

"That's what Socrates did?" asked Billy.

"Yes," answered Thalia, firmly. "He usually took the opposite viewpoint, even if he agreed with you. Even if a solution were the absolutely best solution, Socrates would try to find something wrong with it. He was annoying. He was ready to question anything and everything. Actually, he made a nuisance of himself. He had many enemies and sometimes those who first agreed with him, would later be opponents of his. He was hard to pin down to any rule or regulation."

"He was a teacher and he attracted many young people to him," she went on. "There were many times when the parents of his students strongly objected to what Socrates was teaching their young ones."

"This went on for many years," said Thalia. "And, finally, when he was an old man, a group of citizens decided to prosecute him, charging him with refusing to recognize the gods of the state, but they had also in mind skewering him for his anti-democratic teachings. In ancient Athens, citizens could bring such charges against someone."

"This happened in 399 B. C., when he was already an old man, seventy years old! He was tried before a jury of five hundred citizens!" said Thalia, "right there in the heart of the city!"

"Well, here we are at the doctor's office," said Billy. "I'm now convinced, you've convinced me, that I should try to dream about the trial of Socrates in ancient Greece."

Billy's participation in the doctor's experiments was to allow himself to be put under hypnosis. Several times, in earlier sessions, the doctor had made Billy unconscious, and he was getting used to this action. He usually called this "being put to sleep" or "going off to dreamland" or just "sleeping" or "dreaming".

As his medical specialty, Dr. Dulcamara was making studies of the effects of hypnosis on Billy. He was seeking to determine what medical uses could be instituted by using this new, specialized technique, this hypnosis.

"Hello, doctor," said Billy, as he and Thalia entered the office. "Here we are, ready to participate in another experiment."

"And," chimed in Thalia, as the doctor took her hat, "we have another ancient hero to contact. We hope that Billy, when he's asleep, will find himself in ancient Greece."

"Ancient Greece!" exclaimed the doctor. "And which person or event is he hoping to connect with?"

"With the trial of Socrates," answered Thalia, with reassurance. For several days prior, she had been coaching Billy about Socrates, feeding him full of information about the man, his friends, democracy in Greece, and so forth.

"Ah, that's very well known to me," answered the doctor, with enthusiasm. "Yes, Socrates—one of the most important men to live during ancient Greek times. You've hit on a subject that I'm familiar with."

"Socrates," said Dr. Dulcamara, "brought the concept of religion down from the heavens. Prior to him, all Greeks blamed their actions on the gods. He made the individual responsible. He spoke about the soul and the individual's management of his soul and of every man's own personal righteousness towards his fellow man."

"He was the first well-known Greek philosopher who put responsibility onto the individual," he added. "Following him were Plato and Aristotle. But Socrates led the way!"

"Well, I'm full of information about Socrates," laughed Billy, looking directly at Thalia to give her a thankful nod. "If I get to know any more about that fellow, I'm afraid that I will burst!" he said as he pushed out his chest and stomach as if the information had added weight to his slender frame.

"Good, Good!" exclaimed Dr. Dulcamara. "I hope that you can connect with that great man. I'm nearly ready. Just take your place and make any last minute preparatory changes. I'll be right there in a few moments."

The doctor attended to a few things while Billy took a seat on the sofa and, with Thalia's help, leaned back against the enormous pillows. Thalia found a chair and brought it close to the sofa. She whispered a few words in Billy's ear.

"Now, Billy," said the doctor, as he turned to his patient, "I want you to hold this paper and stare at the first sentence. If you wish, you can read the sentence aloud. Or you can just read it to yourself, silently. As you read it, try to think of the pleasantness of the day—that the sun is shining, there is no rain, it is warm and there are many people walking about in the center of the town."

Boom! As soon as the doctor said *many people ... in the center of the town*, Billy nodded off. He slowly relaxed against the pillows and was in his dream-like state.

Billy found himself among a great many people, maybe a thousand. They were in the agora part of Athens. He moved close to two men.

"Crito," said Phaedo, "where is the master?"

"He's coming along," answered Crito, "He'll be here any minute. As you well know, you cannot hurry Socrates. He has a pace of his own and he will go at that pace even if an elephant is charging down on him."

"Yes," laughed Phaedo, heartily, "how well I know Socrates and his ability to go at his pace. Sometimes that gets a bit annoying, but how can you change a man who is already in his seventies?" You may try, but I'll never attempt it—it's useless to change him in any way!"

"Here he comes now," said Crito, as he saw Socrates emerge from a group of men. Alongside Socrates were several of his companions, walking with him to show their support.

Socrates slowly moved toward the center area, greeting this person and that person along the way. This was an unusually large crowd of Athenians.

Socrates took a seat at the front of the crowd. He was the accused one, the centerpiece of this drama. Three citizens, all accusers of Socrates, next entered the central area. They were the accusers. Each side was allotted three hours to present their case—prosecution and defense.

The first accuser spoke to the crowd for five minutes. Then the second accuser spoke for the same amount of time, followed by the third accuser.

After the third citizen had spoken for five minutes, the first citizen arose and spent at least forty-five minutes detailing how Socrates had refused to recognize the Athenian gods. Following that speaker, the second accuser spoke for nearly an hour, telling stories about how Socrates taught his students to ignore the Athenian gods.

Finally, the third accuser spoke, dwelling on Socrates' effect on the students, teaching them wrongly and corrupting them so that they would never become effective citizens of Athens.

"Now it is his turn," said Crito to Phaedo, "We'll hear from the master, himself."

While Socrates stood and walked to the podium, Billy listened to some comments of the crowd. Within this crowd of citizens, a unit of five hundred, had been chosen to act as the jury.

The jury would vote on the verdict after each side had spoken. Voting was done by each juror putting a ceramic piece, either white-colored or dark-colored, into a large jar. When they finished voting, the pieces would be counted to determine the guilt or innocence of the accused person.

"They didn't make much of a case against him," Billy heard one man say. "Every young man is corrupted in some way. He either drinks too much or is a womanizer, or both. That's been true for ages."

"Yes," his friend said, "but you left out gambling. Many young men are ruined early by gambling."

"Yes," another man added. "Look at those young men who drink too much. Who supplies them the wine? Who urges them to drink it? Which merchants are getting rich by helping our youth become our drunken youth?"

"Nay," said a third man. "That's not the case. This case has nothing to do with drinking, gambling, or womanizing. The problem lies with Socrates. He is a well-known teacher and the teacher molds the man. Our youth must revere our gods and must obey our rules. Socrates is leading them astray. He's putting wrong ideas into their minds. They're too young to know the difference. I say send Socrates off into exile; we don't want him here in Athens any longer."

"Hush," said one man, "he's about to speak."

Socrates first said that he would sit while he spoke, due to his seventy years. It was too hard on him to stand while he addressed the crowd. He told a number of stories in his own defense but none of what he said seemed to be effective. The jury was polite but they did not seem convinced.

"He's just rambling on," said one of the citizens in the crowd. "He's not making any special points in his own defense, he's very ineffective."

After about two hours, Socrates thanked the crowd for listening to him and he walked back to his seat.

The jury began to vote and when the votes were counted, Socrates had lost. He was found guilty by a vote of 280 to 220.

"That was a lot closer than I thought it would be," said Crito to Phaedo. "I thought he'd lose by a much wider margin."

"Yes," replied Phaedo, "he didn't do himself any good when he spoke to the crowd. It seemed like he didn't care if they found him guilty or not guilty. Why do you suppose he presented that type of defense?"

"I can only guess," said Crito. "And, my guess is that he's tired of the whole business. He just doesn't care whether he stays in Athens or is exiled or whatever his fate is to be. He just doesn't seem to care."

The Jury Foreman addressed the crowd: "By a vote of 280 to 220 the defendant, Socrates, is found guilty of the charges that were brought against him. Now we will conduct the penalty phase of the trial. I ask the jurors to discuss this among themselves and, in one hour's time, to render to me what the punishment shall be."

"You can decide on several courses," he said. "First, that Socrates be exiled from Athens. Second, that he be put to death. Third, that another course be taken. Now, it is in your hands."

Various groups formed to discuss the punishment. Billy listened to one group, then moved to another group to hear their discussions. After an hour, the Jury Foreman asked the group what they had decided on.

"We find," said one of the appointed fellows, "that Socrates, who was found guilty of the charges, be exiled from Athens at once."

"Socrates," said the Jury Foreman, "you've heard the punishment. What say you as to your punishment?"

Socrates slowly advanced to the rostrum.

"My punishment?" he asked, as if dumbfounded. "Why, I should be rewarded for all of my good efforts!"

"Now, sire," said the Foreman, "be reasonable. You can't be found guilty of crimes and expect to receive a reward. Come, come, tell us your measure of punishment."

"Well," replied the old man, "I think I should be fined one mina. That appears to me to be sufficient."

Quickly, Crito rushed over and spoke to Socrates.

"Sir," said Socrates, "I meant to say a fine of thirty mina."

The crowd began to hoot and holler. "Thirty mina—a mere pittance", someone in the crowd shouted. It was no heavy financial punishment at all. A few in the crowd applauded; they were probably the ones who had voted for acquittal.

"Now, now, master," said the Foreman. "You must get serious about this matter. Please, tell us your choice, either exile or death!"

"Oh," groaned Crito, who had returned to stand near Phaedo. He reacted when he heard the word *death*. "That's the word I didn't want to hear. I'm afraid that Socrates will take them up on that."

"Exile doesn't appeal to me," said Socrates, almost nonchalantly. "I've been an Athenian for all of my seventy years. I will not take up citizenship in another state. Give me the death sentence."

"No, No!" was heard in the crowd, which appeared to be restless. Maybe there would be a riot or an uprising. This was an important issue and an important man. The Foreman paused until calm was restored. The crowd waited the sentence that Socrates would suffer.

"Let me be sure that I understand you," said the Foreman. "You are willing to receive death as your punishment?"

"Oh, yes," said Socrates. "My time is ending. I'm an old man. There is not much use in these bones, in this body, in this person standing before you. It is time for me to go."

"All right," said the Foreman, with a final gesture. "You have pronounced your own punishment and it is death. You must now go to the jail and the sentence will be carried out as soon as possible."

The crowd began to disperse. Many in the crowd did not like the sentence of death. Others didn't seem to care; he was an old man, maybe it was time for him to go.

Socrates willingly marched on to the jail. It was expected that he would die the next day. But there was a delay: a sacred ship had been sent to the island of Delos and no one could be executed until the ship returned. Socrates would wait in jail until that ship returned. He stays there overnight.

The next morning, Socrates eats breakfast and soon after, is visited by his friends. He spends the next days in jail, visited by friends and happily enjoying life. Finally, one early morning, the ship docks at Piraeus.

News of the ship's arrival quickly reaches Socrates and his friends. He now had to make preparations to die.

"I want no women here," said Socrates, to everyone in general. "The women weep too much. I need sturdy men with me, men who will understand my responsibility, my sentence. I'll take the hemlock and obey the dictates that have been given to me. In fact, it is my duty to obey the rules of the state."

"He is destined to die," said Crito to Phaedo, out of earshot of Socrates. "He will do the deed; he will die today. And, he can even say that it's his obligation, as a good citizen, to obey the sentence that was given to him, the death sentence."

"Yes," replied Phaedo, "it's hard for me to believe that I am seeing the last of good Socrates. It moves me too much. I may have to leave before he drinks the poison."

"You can't leave," insisted Crito. "What if he needs something? What if he asks for you? You can't leave. None of us can leave. We all must stay and witness this solemn, tragic event."

Meanwhile, Billy Costello, had entered the jail cell area to observe what was to transpire. He said nothing, simply standing in the background, out of the way. He wanted to see what was happening but he did not want to be part of any of this affair, this suicide of Socrates.

"My friends," said Socrates, "I am ready."

Crito walked over to a slave boy and whispered something to him. The boy dashed away. A few minutes later, he came back, along with a tall, gaunt man who held a beaker of liquid, the death-poison.

The tall man walked over to Socrates.

"You are the man called Socrates?" he asked, although he knew him well. Everyone knew Socrates. The man just wanted to carry out his duty of insuring that the hemlock liquid poison was given to the right person.

"I am, and a little bit proud of it," smiled Socrates.

"Oh," quietly moaned Phaedo, silently to himself, as he buried his head in his hands, "I can't stand this. He is joyful just before he is to die! Oh Gods! Give me strength. Give me the same strength as noble Socrates is showing to us, give me that iron will to do what is to be done. I feel faint but I must stay strong. I must give my beloved friend my full support."

"Crito," he said, "did you just hear what Socrates said?"

"Yes," replied Crito, tears swelling in his eyes. "He is ready, he is resigned to his death. He is so strong." He bowed his head and said a silent prayer.

The gaunt man handed the cup of hemlock to Socrates and then stepped back about two paces.

"My good man," said Socrates, "tell me how this is supposed to work. How am I to drink it—by sips, or all at once?"

"You should drink it straight down," replied the gaunt man. "Do not hesitate. Just gulp it down. That is the best way."

"And," said Socrates, calmly, "after it is in me, what are the symptoms that will appear?"

"After you drink it, walk around a little and you will feel heaviness in your legs," replied the gaunt man, very precisely and with an air showing that he had performed this service many times before. "Your legs will soon be weak and you'll need to sit or lie down, probably lying down is best. When you have lain down, you will soon feel the full effect of it."

Feeling the full effect of it meant that Socrates would fall asleep—a sleep from which he'd never again waken.

"Apollodorus," said Crito, as he edged over to another of Socrates' close friends, "did you hear that from the cup-bearer? What are we to do?"

Socrates has drunk the poison

"Oh, Crito," replied Apollodorus, tears running down his cheeks, "I'm so wrought with terrible feelings. It is a punishment indeed for me, to watch my dearest friend, give his life this day. How I wish I could change things!"

"This is his wish, you know," said Crito. "He had the opportunity to choose exile from Athens, but he would not take that. He insisted on dying."

"Why? Why? Why would our beloved, dear friend, want to die, to leave us, taking away his wisdom and knowledge, leaving us bare of his guidance and discussions?" replied Apollodorus.

"Apollodorus, my friend," said Phaedo, as he came to the two men. "There is no answer to your question. Our beloved master has decided that this will be his final day on Earth and we must accept it. We must accept it with tears streaming down from our eyes."

Socrates looked over at the three men. "Why are you weeping?" he asked. "There is something strange going on here. I asked that no women be present because I did not want weeping and now, there you are, three good friends of mine, with tears running down your cheeks."

"Now, my friends," added Socrates. "Get hold of yourselves and no more weeping. Rejoice with me. I need you to be quiet and to control your persons."

With that he took the cup and drained it fully. After drinking, he handed the cup to the young boy who stood next to the gaunt man.

"I will walk a little as you suggest," he said to the tall man, "and I'll follow your instructions."

As Socrates walked, he stopped occasionally to converse with some one. Billy watched him closely. After a few minutes, he said: "My legs are beginning to feel heavy, I think I'll sit down on the bed."

Shortly after sitting on the bed, he decided to lie down. Some pillows were propped behind the back of his head. He motioned to Crito.

Crito walked over to Socrates and reached for his hand.

"Crito, I promised to give a cock to Asclepius, but I've not kept my promise so far. Please carry out my obligation to him. Don't forget."

Crito nodded assent. He released his hand. Socrates closed his eyes. Someone handed him a damp cloth and he put it over his eyes and his forehead.

Crito still stood by the bed, unable to move away. He closely watched his friend. He thought his breathing was becoming more shallow. He stepped back a pace, still observing his friend.

Suddenly, Socrates' body shook slightly. The tall, gaunt man came over and uncovered his forehead. He pushed back the eyelids and looked into his eyes.

"My duty is done," he said, as he turned to the group, and began to walk away. The slave boy went with him.

Billy, tears in his eyes, watched the friends of Socrates huddle together in small groups. They sobbed and groaned. Billy wanted to get out into the fresh air, so he turned and left the jail-cell area.

Just as he came out of the building he felt a hand on his arm and, looking up, he saw the face of Thalia, his wife. She was smiling at him, as he gradually regained consciousness from being under Dr. Dulcamara's hypnosis.

"Sweetheart," said Thalia, gently. "Did you get back to ancient Greece? Did you see Socrates?"

"Oh, yes!" replied Billy, as he gained more and more awareness. "I was there. Socrates was there, Crito was there, and others connected to Socrates. It was a really good show, I'll tell you."

"But," he added, "it was terribly sad. I was deeply moved. I just can't tell you how sorry I am about that whole trial and suicide thing. I feel awful."

"So," said Thalia, more seriously, "you did see the trial and him drinking the hemlock poison?"

"Yes, yes," answered Billy, while Dr. Dulcamara quickly scribbled notes about this event. "The trial was kind of strange. Socrates didn't seem to be concerned if he was guilty or not guilty. He knew he was not guilty or so he said, but he refused to be exiled. He chose death instead."

"How can any man choose death over exile?" he asked no one in particular. "I just can't understand that part."

"That's been a question for ages," said Dr. Dulcamara. "It's never been fully explained, to my satisfaction, that Socrates preferred death to exile. He would have been welcome in many other city-states, but he elected not to go away from Athens. Why?"

"This is going to be in my mind for a good many days to come," said Billy. "Maybe there is no answer to it, but I'll be thinking about it for a long time."

Chapter 10

Johannes Gutenberg

"Printing?" exclaimed Billy. "Yes, I can see the importance of printing. But what makes Johannes Gutenberg so famous, so much a hero of history?"

"Well," said his wife, Thalia. "Everything that is important begins small, begins as a very small change or a very small idea. Then it grows in importance."

"Sometimes," she added, "the idea is already there and the new guy adds something to it. He makes a minor change and Voila!—there is a new path taken. It amounts to a new invention, and he gets credit for it."

"So, Gutenberg, was the guy?" asked Billy. "He was the fellow who was ready when the time came for him to act and he did act."

"You've got it," replied Thalia, as they continued their walk toward Dr. Dulcamara's office. They were helping the doctor study his new medical procedure, called hypnotism. He would place Billy into an unconsciousness stage and then study his actions and responses while he was asleep. The doctor had already given Billy several sessions, put him to sleep and made studies of him.

Before Billy was put to sleep he had prepared himself to dream, to imagine that he was present at some historic event. It had worked each time and this time he hoped to go back in history to when Johannes Gutenberg developed printing, as we know it in the Western World.

"Well, here we are," said Thalia, enthusiastically, as they arrived at the doctor's office. She opened the door and they walked in.

"Hello to my two favorite clients," laughed Dr. Dulcamara, as he came forward and shook their hands. "Welcome, welcome to this new session. I hope that you are ready."

"Ready and willing," laughed Billy. "We've picked out a subject and Thalia has been coaching me for several days now, so I'm prepared, well prepared."

"And, your subject is?" queried the doctor.

"Johannes Gutenberg, the originator or inventor of movable-type printing," replied Billy with gusto.

"Ah, a good choice, a very good choice," replied the doctor, happily glad that they'd chosen a person whose history he was familiar with.

"I know about Gutenberg," he said. "The story is familiar to me. I made a personal study of him when I was a student, so I'm glad that you will try to visit that event—when he created or invented movable type."

"In fact," said the doctor, "I have some notes that I made about him years ago. Hold on a minute," he said as he began searching a bookshelf.

"Ah, there it is," he said as he removed a notebook from deep behind some medical books. As he walked towards Billy he thumbed through the pages of his notebook.

"Yes!" he said, triumphantly. "These are the notes I made about Johannes Gutenberg. Here is a list of his problems."

The doctor recited from his earlier notes:

He was born around 1398, probably in Mainz, Germany.

He had started out as a goldsmith or a metal-smith.

His family was well-to-do and they had to move from their home in Mainz when some riots occurred.

About 1439, he was involved in a financial bust. He and his partners were making mirrors that they claimed would capture holy light when they reflected various religious relics. They offered these for sale to pilgrims who were visiting Aachen. The mirrors were sold to believers, who thought they would reflect good effects on the buyer, since the mirror had reflected various relics. It was a stretch to believe that the mirrors had any curative value.

Much of Gutenberg's early life is unknown and must be guessed at, so there is no firm evidence of what he did or didn't do.

Apparently about 1440, when he was 42, he tinkered around and perfected his system for printing with movable type.

About 1448 he was again in Mainz, his original home, and there he borrowed money from Arnold Gelthus. Apparently, he was getting ready to set up a printing press. Some records indicate that his press was operating in 1450 and he borrowed more money, this time from Johann Fust, a moneylender.

Now Gutenberg was planning to print the Bible, a tremendous undertaking and during this time it seemed, according to some people, that he'd bitten off too much to chew. The moneylender wanted to be repaid and there were other problems. By 1455 this dispute went to court and Gutenberg lost—he was effectively bankrupt!

But, he opened another shop and he got the Bible printed although he was only one member of a team. But he was the most important member, although the printed Bibles did not carry anyone's name including his. He was involved in printing 180 Bibles, a huge amount.

"There," said the doctor, "my student notes have helped you get more information about Johannes Gutenberg."

"My goodness!" exclaimed Billy. "You must have been a fine student, considering that you wrote down all of those notes about only one man! I'm impressed."

"Yes," laughed the doctor. "Sometimes we students wonder if our studies will ever have any meaning and this is one case where the meaning fits."

"But," said Dr. Dulcamara, "we must get on with our session. We can talk more about Herr Gutenberg later."

"I'm ready," said Billy, as he sat on the couch and, with Thalia's help, arranged some pillows for him to lean against.

"All right," said the doctor. "Now, I want you to watch my hand as it moves slowly in front of you. Keep watching it, keep watching it."

Suddenly Billy found himself in Mainz, Germany. He was walking on the street and he stopped in front of a printing shop. He looked in the window and decided to go inside.

"Yes, sir," asked the counter person, "what can I do for you, sir?"

"I'm interested in the printing process," answered Billy. "May I watch it in operation?"

"Of course," replied the man. "Come with me."

They walked to the rear of the shop. There, five men were in the process of printing pages.

"Herr Gutenberg," said the counter person, as he pointed to Billy, "this man wants to watch the printing process."

"Yes, yes," said Johannes Gutenberg, a bit impatiently. "Stand right over there. We're involved with a delicate operation now and I will talk more with you later. You can watch what we're doing."

"Thank you, sir," acknowledged Billy, as he stood in an area that seemed to not interfere with anything that any of the men was doing.

Billy watched closely as one man laid a sheet of paper on a receiving plate. Another plate, containing type, came down towards it. As they got close, the paper was moved directly under the type. The arm with the type sat directly against the paper and a screw-type device forced it down hard. Two men handled the arms of the screw-type device as they squeezed it hard against the paper.

Quickly, the pressure was released and the screw-type press was lifted away from the paper. Herr Gutenberg carefully picked up the paper and examined it. He nodded his approval and laid it on a nearby shelf.

They repeated the process and he laid another printed sheet on a nearby shelf. After several times, he directed his assistant to move into his position and do what he'd been doing.

"So, you see, sir," said Gutenberg, as he came over to stand with Billy, "we very carefully print each page in the manner that you just watched. If we intend to make fifty books, we'll print fifty of each page; then we'll print fifty of the next page, and so on.

"Each time that we have our fifty pages," he added, "we'll have the type set for the next page and then make fifty of the next page. As each page is being made, someone is preparing the type for the next page. That way we use our time more effectively."

"That seems like a very ingenuous method," said Billy.

"Yes, it is," replied Johannes, modestly. "But anyone can do it if they just lay out their plans properly."

"Ah, there's the rub," laughed Billy. "That "if" in there separates the men from the boys. If anyone prepares his plans and follows his plans."

"Yes, that's true," said the printer. "That's true of every mechanical operation. You must lay out your plans, prepare your work, and follow your preparations."

"Also," he added, "often you cannot do everything yourself so you must find assistants who can do what you would do. They must be able to substitute for you. Many operators do not want anyone to replace them, but they can't do it all, they can't do everything, they must hire competent helpers."

"How do you prepare your type?" asked Billy, trying not to be too inquisitive, but anxious to know more about this wonderful process.

Johannes Gutenberg explains his printing press to Billy

"I've developed a special method," replied Johannes, as he picked up several letters that would be used. "You can see that each letter, and each punctuation mark, is an entity unto itself. And, they're all the same size—that's so they will fit in the holder, with their surfaces on an equal plane."

"We simply put the type into this holder," added Johannes. "Then we bind it tightly and it's ready to be used, to make a full page. Here are some moveable type that we use."

Moveable type letters

"As I see it," said Billy, with a laugh, "the person who prepares the type, I guess you call him the typesetter, must be able to read backwards."

"Oh, yes," chuckled Johannes, "that's a requirement. Look over there and you'll see that we have some mirrors to help the typesetter. But, you may be surprised, a typesetter very quickly learns to read sentences backwards. It comes as part of the trade."

Just then, an assistant brought over a newly-printed page for Johannes to examine. He looked very closely at it, then nodded his assent and handed it back to the assistant.

"I have good men working for me," said Johannes, as he waved his arm towards his co-workers. "I train them and then I trust them. They do my job just like I'd do it myself."

"And," asked Billy, "what is this project that you are now working on?"

"Well, yesterday," replied Johannes, "we finished three thousand indulgences for the Church. As you may know, those indulgences are sold to the church members. They will save them years in Purgatory. The more they buy and own, the more years they save. The Church makes money and the parishioner saves punishment time."

"Now that we've finished that job," he added, "we are started on the Holy Book, the Bible. I intend to print 180 Bibles. It is a massive undertaking but not for me," he said without seeming to inflate his ego.

"I know how to do such a gigantic job," he said, self-assuredly, but without boasting. "It takes a man with a mind that can manage every tiny element of the production, from purchasing the paper and bindings, to do the final binding of the finished product."

"And, of course," he added with a hearty laugh. "Someone, perhaps me, has to make the sale in the first place. Then he gets a down payment or a full payment or he has to borrow some money to produce the goods. It's a complicated job."

"But you seem very capable," said Billy, somewhat admiringly. "You know all the facets involved. You must have spent years developing this process, this production so that it goes off without a hitch."

"That's true," replied Johannes, "I do know everything about this operation since I started many years ago. It took me several years, and lots of experiments, to finalize this type of operation, this production. I'm keenly aware of where the mistakes may occur and I watch that area closely. Once something is printed and bound, it's very costly, and a big job, to unbind the book and replace each page that has an error on it. That's an easy way to lose money and time."

"Sir," said one of his assistants, "we need you. We're over at the typesetting area and we can't decide which is the way you want this done."

"Excuse me," said Johannes to Billy, "I must attend to my duty."

Billy bowed to Johannes as he quickly walked over to another part of the shop, to supervise the typesetting. He soon returned.

"I'm sorry," said Johannes, "I must leave you. I need to more closely supervise this operation."

"My deep thanks to you, Herr Gutenberg," said Billy, with a grateful smile. "I'll be on my way. You've been most helpful to me in explaining your printing process."

Billy took one last look at the printing operation, then turned and walked out through the storefront and onto the street. He paused for a moment, trying to decide which way to go. Suddenly, he felt a hand on his arm and realized that Dr. Dulcamara was gently bringing him back to awareness.

"Did you see Johannes Gutenberg?" asked the doctor.

"Oh, yes!" exclaimed Billy. "What a nice man. He spoke to me and explained the process that he was developing. I was allowed to watch the whole thing. It was marvelous."

"Did he talk about his past?" asked the doctor.

"No," answered Billy, slowly but gradually gaining a firm grip on where he now was. "There was nothing said about anything before the actual time that I was there in his shop, watching him print pages and pages of a new book."

"Well, I have a few more notes to tell you about," said Dr. Dulcamara. "I have a short summary here, near the end of my notes. This recap says that Gutenberg was the first person to develop a practical system using three things: (1)

moveable type, (2) oil-based inks, using vegetable oils, and (3) a screw-driven olive press.

"As a final note," said the doctor, "in 1465, when he was sixty-seven years old, he was given the title **Hofmann** which means **gentleman**. That was a special award and it pleased him greatly."

"He died three years later, in 1468," added the doctor, "and he was buried in a churchyard in Mainz, but that church and the yard were destroyed, so his grave is lost."

"But, his gift to humanity," said the doctor, "was an ever-lasting one. When I was a student, I gave a report on this great man and I declared him and his invention as being the greatest invention in the past 500 years!"

"You were right to make that declaration," said Thalia. "He was the man who provided books and reading to the masses. Prior to his time all books were made by hand or by using wood-blocks to print with. Gutenberg even invented a metal alloy and a special mold to hold the type. I tell you, he was a real genius."

"Now, now, now," said Billy, somewhat annoyed. "You've both had your turn telling about Johannes Gutenberg, but I'm the only one, among the three of us, who he actually talked to! Don't forget that while I was in dreamland, he spoke with me. He showed me the whole operation and described what was going on at the time that I was watching the operation."

"So," he added, as he laughed, "if either of you want any first-hand information about this great man, just ask me!"

They all had a good laugh at that and Dr. Dulcamara invited them to stay and have a cup of tea.

Chapter 11

Martin Luther

"Well, my good friends, Thalia and Billy," said Dr. Dulcamara, as the two entered his office. "We're all set for another session, another experiment."

"All set, doctor," said Billy, as he removed his hat and jacket. His wife, Thalia, placed Billy's hat and jacket and her coat on the pegs on the wall.

"Have you thought of trying to reach back in history to be with another important person?" asked the doctor.

"Yes," answered Billy. "It's one of my favorite heroes. A very brave man named Martin Luther who founded the Protestant Church movement, beginning in about 1517, in what was then Germany."

"Oh, a fine, fine choice," said the doctor. "I hope you can reach him. He was a towering figure and, as you say, he was a very, very brave man. When he opposed the teaching of the Catholic Church, he was marked for death. That Church did not permit anyone to think and act differently from them. Several others, years before Luther, were burned at the stake because they proclaimed a difference of opinion with Rome. Luther knew that he, too, might lose his life when he decided to publicly urge that changes should be discussed."

"Martin Luther didn't want to leave the Catholic Church," said Thalia. "He wanted only to help the Church by suggesting the Church discuss some policy changes that he found to be too extreme. The selling of indulgences was the key practice that Martin Luther wanted to debate, to discuss. But the Roman Church would have none of that. They pounced right on him and if he had not found some German prince to protect him, he'd have met a quick, fiery end."

"Are you ready?" asked the doctor. Billy had sat himself on the sofa and he and Thalia had adjusted the large pillows so that he would recline on them when he entered dreamland. The doctor would hypnotize Billy and he'd be in what he called dreamland for about twenty or thirty minutes.

"Now, Billy," said the doctor, "I want you to look at this sheaf of papers that I'm holding and imagine that you are counting them. Start with the top one and count it, then the next one, and so on. Keep staring at the pile of papers and quietly count to yourself the numbers."

Billy stared at the papers and silently counted but when he got up to four, he suddenly found himself in a medieval town.

"Pardon me," said Billy to a man who had just crossed the street. "Could you direct me to the church?"

"Oh yes, my good man," said the pedestrian. "Over there, then turn right for a short walk, and you'll see it on your left side."

Billy thanked the man and then walked the short distance to the Castle Church. He walked around the church and entered a side door. Inside, he slowly walked along the corridor, then sat in a quiet area. He noticed a short stout man walking nearby who was about to be greeted by another man. They stood and talked just about ten feet from where Billy sat.

"Martin Luther," said his fellow-priest, with a bright laugh, "what in the world do you have there? It looks like you've just collected a sheaf of papers."

Martin Luther had just met his colleague, Frans Holter, in the vast spaces of the Castle Church in Wittenberg, Germany. Frans and he had studied together for the priesthood in the Roman Catholic Church and were longtime, close friends.

"Yes," answered Martin, seriously, "it is a sheaf of papers. But, these papers list ninety-five themes. You may call them theses or debate topics."

"For goodness sakes," queried his colleague, "why have you made a list of debate topics?"

"It's not just any list, dear Frans," answered Luther, "this is a list of subjects that I want to see debated within our Church. I've had it up to my eyebrows with this indulgence thing and there is a pressing need to have it argued about and decided upon. Most of these theses deal with the indulgences."

"But, Martin," exclaimed his friend, "you are skating on very thin ice. Those indulgences are part of Rome's need to pay for debts they've incurred. And, don't forget, Archbishop Albert of Mainz, who slipped deeply in debt in order to buy his high rank in the Church—he gets a cut of the sale of each indulgence sold in his territory."

"You are," he continued, "taking on the Holy See in Rome and the Archbishop in Mainz. They are very strong opponents and will crush you like a mouse under a wagon wheel."

"I can't help it," replied Martin. "I must do what I must do. I've prayed long and hard over this matter and it is my duty to oppose the sale of these indulgences. Indulgences are given freely by God to any parishioner, they need not be bought. In fact, they should not be sold or bought."

"An indulgence," he continued, "is a free gift from God, through our Savior, Jesus Christ. I'm outraged that our Church would sell something that is freely given by God! That's what our Bible teaches us."

Martin seemed to run out of breath as he said that, and he sat on the edge of a low wall as he finished.

"But, Martin, my dear friend," replied Frans, soberly. "You must not do this. You will be crushed. You may be right and they may be wrong, but they will crush you. They have absolute power! They will not tolerate this transparency, they will not welcome any opposition to their practice, no matter how wrong they may be."

"Oskar," said Frans to another colleague who had just joined them, "what do you think of the Church's practice of selling indulgences?"

"I haven't given it much thought," replied Oskar Heim. "In all my priestly duties, I simply follow what I'm told to do and that's that."

"You see," said Martin, "what Oskar has just said, there's part of the trouble. We should not just follow what we're told to do. We must examine what we are ordered to do. In fact, we must continuously examine our efforts. We must feel that whatever we do would be what Jesus would do if he were in our place."

"Martin," said Oskar, anxious to learn what Martin and Frans had been discussing, "what is it now? What are you up to, my good friend?"

"I'll answer for him," replied Frans. "He's getting ready to post some notices on the church door, urging that a debate should take place in regard to the indulgences now being considered for sale here in Saxony."

"Well," answered Oskar, "that's the place to post anything. It's the community bulletin board. But why are you asking for a debate about indulgences, Martin?"

"It's simple," replied Martin. "Indulgences are granted by God, through Jesus Christ, for our sins. They are not to be bought and sold. It's as simple as that!"

"But our Mother Church, our Pope and our Cardinals, in Rome, are telling us that selling indulgences is all right, the proper thing to do," responded Oskar, "so how can you speak against that authority?"

"Well," answered Martin, "in the first place, I think that they are wrong. And, that they are wrong according to our Holy Word, the Bible. Secondly, there is a lot of back-room dealing going on with the sale of these indulgences. True, they're not openly sold here in Saxony, but people travel a little farther to buy them."

"Just the other day," he continued, "I saw a man who had paid cash in real hard silver and, by that means, he had reduced his time in purgatory by nearly five thousand years! I call that crazy and I say that is wrong!"

"You may say it is wrong," said Oskar. "And, Frans and I both can believe you, but what will happen then. We three will be brought into the ecclesiastical court and condemned for heresy—that's what will happen!"

"Heresy—ha," said Martin. "We all know that heresy is simply believing something different from the established beliefs. It's just a difference of opinion. It's not terrible or sinful to believe differently."

"Oh, yes it is!" emphasized Oskar, as Frans shook his head in agreement. "We are not allowed to think differently from what we're told by our superiors. Otherwise, we're committing a sin, a grievous sin! How can we be priests in our Holy Catholic Church if we are heretics?"

"Well," answered Martin, somewhat resignedly, "If we can do only what is told to us to do, that makes us slaves. I don't want to be a slave, do you?"

"No, no, no," answered Oskar, "we're not slaves. We can do what we're told or we can leave the priesthood. The choice is in our hands."

"And," said Martin, smiling, "you do not see the slavery aspect to your calling, to your being a priest? Let me pose a question: have you ever been asked, by any Church superior, for your opinion about how the Church conducts itself?"

"Well, no," answered Oskar. "I've never been asked."

"Do you know anybody who's ever been asked by the Church for his opinion?" continued Martin.

"No, I haven't," replied Oskar. Frans shook his head in agreement.

"Doesn't that tell you something?" asked Martin. "Does it take a deep-thinking philosopher to reason out the methods of our Church's conduct? No! There is a time to stand up and debate the methods of our operations, to consider going back to the Bible and following its directions."

"We've gotten too worldly," he continued. "And, these indulgences are proof of that. We've lost sight of saving souls. We've lost sight of sheltering the poor and needy. We need to re-examine our practices and we can begin by discussing and debating these indulgences."

"You know, Oskar," said Frans, "Martin is right. We have gotten too worldly. We do need to bring everything out into the daylight and examine our practices."

"Oh, don't be foolish," said Oskar, emphatically. "I love you and Martin. You are both dear to me. You are my brothers. But you will be burnt at the stake if you try to get our superiors to debate this topic, this indulgence thing."

"Martin is a wonderful man and a good priest," continued Oskar. "But, he is argumentative. Now, I think that is good because it helps keep our direction, as priests, going forward. But, he can't be argumentative with the Church leaders—they won't stand for it. They dictate to us and we do as they tell us to do."

"Martin will argue at the drop of a hat or, if there is no hat available, at the drop of anything!" he went on, with a chuckle, "and he is a deep thinker. He will bring to any argument the points that are important, the points that should be discussed. I admire him greatly." He reached over and gave Martin a friendly pat on the shoulder.

"And," said Frans, "he has always been concerned with the individual person. One person at a time suits him well. Each individual is important to Martin."

"Yes, I suppose so," replied Luther, smiling but serious. "I can't help taking the side of the individual. I must stand up for the human being and his rights, the right for him to conduct himself as he believes to be right."

"But, there's a problem," said Frans. "The individual doesn't know right from wrong. He needs guidance from people who will represent him before God. That's what our Mother Church does—it intercedes between him and God."

"You mean, as if our Church were his agent?" said Luther, with a derisive chuckle. "No way, man. Any thinking man does NOT need anyone to intercede between him and our Lord. He, himself, can connect with our Lord through prayer. That was firmly fixed in our early leaders. But, over the years, the Church has promoted itself as being needed by the individual to clear up any effects of his sin in his lifetime."

"That's where our Father, the Pope, says that you're wrong, decidedly wrong," said Frans, with conviction and sure of himself. "Our entire teaching is based on interceding between the individual and our Lord."

"I may be wrong in the eyes of our Church officials," said Martin, with self-assurance, "but in my own eyes, I'm right! And, that's the principle that we've lost. We've decided that the individual cannot go it alone, that he needs we priests and other church officials to intercede for him. I believe differently from them."

"And, there is the charge of heresy against you," said Oskar. "You've just stated a difference of opinion, a different way for our Mother Church to rule its members. That's heresy!"

"There's more than one good and proper way to govern," said Martin, stroking his chin. "There is the way that the Church has laid out, but who, besides the Church officials, says that way is the only way? If you talk to five farmers, you will hear five ways to run and manage a farm—and they'll all be correct in their way of operation. Why can't our Church consider that? Are they afraid of change?"

"You just hit the nail on the head," exclaimed Frans. "They are afraid of change. Each new Pope, each new Cardinal, has already made up his mind to follow the rules of the predecessors, and they won't change anything. Why? Because they would lose all their benefits."

"You know," he went on, "they lead a nice life. They have a lifetime job, plenty of good food to eat, adequate (sometimes elegant) housing, errand boys and housekeepers and so on. They don't want to change any of that. That's why there will be no change in our lifetime!"

"Friends, friends," said Oskar. "My dear colleagues, we must get off this subject. We have no choice in this matter. We're at the bottom of the pole. We have to do what we're told to do, and that's that!"

"You're right, my good fellows," said Martin. "You both should forget that we've had this discussion. Why? Because I'm going to put these debates, these topics, these theses, all ninety-five of them, on the church door, begging to have them brought to a debate."

"So," he added. "I don't want you two to get into any kind of trouble because of me. I don't want to implicate you two, and that is why I'm suggesting that you both forget what we've just been talking about."

"There may be a big upheaval after I post these on the church's door," he went on, seriously, "and I may be brought to trial for trying to make the Church better. If I am tried, it's best that you two not be part of it. I'm willing, and happy, to go it alone, even though I know that many of my colleagues will give me silent support."

"When are you going to post them?" asked Frans.

"Probably tomorrow morning, or maybe yet today," said Martin. "They're all ready to put there now but I want to make one last review of them before I make them public."

"Well, I wish you the best of luck," said Frans, as he embraced Martin.

"And, me, too," added Oskar, as he shook hands with Martin. "I am afraid of what they will do to you, my good friend. You may lose your life, trying to make the Church a better place. It's happened to others before you."

"Oh, don't worry about me," said Martin, half-heartedly, "I'll win out. Or, if I don't win, I'll find some protection somewhere that I'll be safe."

Billy had sat silently, taking in this entire conversation among these three priests.

The three men split up, with Martin going off to his study to review the notices that he expected to put on the door of the church.

Billy got up from his seat and wandered into the main part of the church. He sat in one of the pews. It was very silent but there was a beauty there. The sunlight streamed through the high-set windows and the church seemed very peaceful. A peace that would soon be shattered by Martin Luther's request to discuss how the church should operate.

Billy thought about the rights of man, of the importance of the individual, of the joy he had, in personally saying his prayers to his God, and feeling close to his Savior. He knew that he could reach out one-on-one to Jesus; he didn't need anyone to be his agent, to intercede for him with Jesus or the Father. He was a thinking man and could follow his own path.

Of course, it was always helpful to have a minister to discuss guidance and rightful living. But, the individual did not need a Master, telling him what to do and what not to do. He did not need someone commanding him to do it a certain way or he'd go to Hell. What he most needed was a friend, a colleague, a brother with deep understanding.

As he sat in the pew, Billy suddenly saw a short, stout man walking towards a rear door. It was Martin Luther.

Billy watched closely as he opened the door and went outside. Billy rose from the pew and went through the same door, to the street, where he saw Martin walking towards the front of the church.

Luther nails the Theses to the church door

Billy stayed far enough back so he would not be noticed as Martin stood in front of the church doors. Quickly, and with no fanfare, Martin affixed the sheets of paper to the church door, the papers that contained the ninety-five theses.

Then, he stood back to see that they were arranged properly and, when satisfied, he quietly left the front of the church and retraced his steps to go through the door at the rear of the building.

After he was out of sight, Billy went to the entrance of the church and saw the papers attached to the door. Several other people came by and read some of the theses. A small crowd began to gather.

Billy turned to go when he felt someone touch his arm. He realized that someone was at his elbow. He looked around to see who it was and there was his wife, Thalia, saying: "Wake up, sweetheart. You've been in dreamland for the past half-hour."

Billy quickly regained consciousness as Thalia and Dr. Dulcamara resettled in their chairs. They were ready to bombard him with questions about his trip.

"Did you reach Martin Luther?" asked Thalia, eagerly.

"Oh, yes," said Billy. "And I saw him post the ninety-five theses on the door of the church at Wittenberg. Also, before he posted the theses, he and two other priests spent a long time talking about them and the reasons that Martin Luther had to bring them to a debate, to a discussion—and I heard it all!"

"I was thrilled," he went on, excitedly, "I was right there, sitting within earshot of the three priests while they discussed what Martin Luther was about to do. It was wonderful!"

"They didn't see you?" asked the doctor.

"No," answered Billy. "I was in a dark area of the church, but I was very near to where they were, and I could hear every word."

"And," said Thalia, eagerly and a bit jealously, "you saw Martin Luther post the theses to the door of the church! What a thrill! Oh, how I wish I had been with you! That would have been a highlight of my life."

The doctor made copious notes as Billy talked. After thirty or forty minutes, it was time to end the session. They said good-bye to Dr. Dulcamara and told him that they would be ready for another experimental session at whatever time he would choose.

As Billy and Thalia walked home, they passed the Lutheran Church. Billy walked over and held the flat of his hand against one of the stones in the foundation. He pushed against it.

"This church is built on a solid foundation," said Billy to Thalia. "I touched that rock as if it were representative of Martin Luther, the brave man who laid the foundation for that church and for most of the Protestant churches, not only in our country but throughout the world."

"I agree," said Thalia, as she edged closer to her husband, feeling his strong presence. "Martin Luther was **the**

man and he liberated the individual. We're free today because of him, perhaps even freer than he imagined."

"Thank God for Martin Luther," exclaimed Billy. "He was the beginning of getting the individual man free of despotism, of overbearing authority. Mind you, he did not set every man free at once, but he was the beginning. Even for years after him, the individual was still subject to overbearing authority but he began the process. Someone had to begin it and he was, as you say, **the man**!"

Chapter 12

Christopher Columbus

"In fourteen hundred and ninety-two, Columbus sailed the ocean blue," laughed Thalia as she walked along with her husband, Billy. They were going to Dr. Dulcamara's office to participate in another session involving hypnosis. The doctor was using Billy as a guinea pig in his experiments.

"Yes, my dear," replied Billy, as he gave her hand a gentle squeeze, "and where would we be today, if Columbus hadn't found this new land?"

"Well," answered Thalia, as she stepped along smartly, "that's a big, big question. I'm sure that it would have been discovered later on, maybe not much later than 1492."

"There are some folks," said Billy, "that say the Norsemen or the Icelanders got here before Columbus. They claim that Eric the Red or Leif Eric or someone like that, reached the New England area long before Columbus."

"Yes," answered Thalia. "I've heard that, too. But nobody seems able to find any evidence to support that belief. It's going to need some newly-found records or some kind of relic or whatever, to substantiate those claims."

"Well, here we are," said Billy, as they arrived at the front door of the doctor's office. "I'm gonna try to connect with old Chris Columbus himself during this session."

"Good for you," exclaimed his wife. "That's the fellow we must stick with. He's the accepted discoverer of America, at least until some one finds proof otherwise. Whether someone else got here before him, we don't know who that was. So, we've got to stick with Columbus."

They walked into the doctor' office just as he came out from an inner room to greet them.

"Hello Thalia and Billy," said Dr. Dulcamara, as he shook hands with each. He was holding a white, clean cloth and using it to dry a glass beaker. "No doubt you've selected an outstanding person for this session, haven't you?"

"Yes," responded Billy. "Tell him, Thalia, what we've decided on."

"Well," said Thalia. "Billy is going to try to connect with Christopher Columbus, about the time of 1492 when he first set foot on land in the New World."

"That's wonderful," enthused the doctor. "I am familiar with some parts of Columbus' career and life. He was a visionary and he had difficulty in getting people, especially highly-placed officials, to agree with his thinking. He insisted that the world was round and that by sailing either East or West, he could reach the Indies."

"Yes, the fabulous Indies," exclaimed Thalia. "That's what intrigued many European explorers."

"But he persevered," said the doctor. "He was a determined man and he kept pushing his ideas until finally they took hold and he was able to get funding for his adventure."

"It must have been a difficult time for him," said Billy. "He had this great idea of sailing West, instead of East, to reach the Indies. But there were many superstitions then. Some people, even well-placed people, thought he would fall off the edge of the earth, kind of like going over a waterfall."

"It seems sort of strange thinking with what we know now," said Thalia. "It's hard to believe that less than five hundred years ago, people believed the world was flat."

"Ha, Ha!" laughed Billy. "Some people today still believe the world is flat. Or, at least, they can't figure out how the world can be round."

"True, true," chimed in Dr. Dulcamara. "But I'm pretty sure that most people today, here in the year 1856, feel that the world is round. At least, I hope they feel that way," he laughed. "It would be a shame if I am proved wrong and lots and lots of people still believe in a flat world."

"Well," said Billy, impatiently, "we better try to get me connected with that great sailor, Columbus. I'm itching to see if I can make contact with him."

"And, so you should be," laughed the doctor.

Billy sat on the sofa and Thalia arranged some large pillows for him to lie back on. He was all ready for his next adventure, hoping to find Columbus in his dreams.

"Now, Billy," said the doctor, as he took a fish bowl from a nearby table, "I want you to look at the fish in this bowl, watch it swim back and forth and keep concentrating on it. Imagine that the water is very deep, maybe it is deep enough to be a real ocean. Keep concentrating, keep concentrating."

Billy stared at the bowl. He watched the fish swim about and suddenly a voice near him asked: "Are you watching those dolphins swimming near us?"

"Yes," replied Billy, as he turned to speak to a sailor named Carlos. "I'm intrigued by how they often stay close to the ship. Do you think they are expecting food from us?"

"No, I don't think so," replied Carlos. "They just want to hang around and see what's going to happen."

"Well, they certainly are good swimmers," said Billy. "I wish I could swim like that."

"Don't we all!" laughed Carlos.

They were joined by Pedro, another sailor on this ship, the *Santa Maria*, one of three that Columbus was using to sail from Spain westwardly to the Indies. Columbus himself captained the *Santa Maria*. The other two ships were the

Nina and the *Pinta*. All three ships were called caravels, small, fast sailing vessels,

"Has anyone told you?" asked Pedro of Carlos.

"About what?" responded Carlos.

"About turning back, back to home," said Pedro, almost in a whisper. "There's a move afoot to have our Captain turn around and go back home."

"But that would destroy our mission!" exclaimed Carlos. "We can't do that!"

"Oh, yes we can," responded Pedro. "We just found out that our Captain has been keeping two sets of logs—one set showing the true distance we've traveled and the other set showing that we've traveled less far."

"Well, what's the meaning of that?" asked Carlos.

"It means, my good sir," replied Pedro, somewhat self-assuredly, "that we're further from home than the Captain wanted to tell us. We may be very near the critical point."

"What's the critical point?" asked Carlos.

"That's when most people say we'll fall off the edge of the earth!" declared Pedro. "We're close to it now and we're getting closer every minute and every hour and every day!"

"That's only true if you believe that the earth is flat," declared Carlos, a bit annoyed. "You people who believe that the earth is flat are not being reasonable. The earth is round. Round, round, I tell you!"

"Do you think I'm gonna listen to a simple sailor like you are?" responded Pedro. "No way, man! You're in league with those scientists, but we real people know the difference in what is and what is supposed to be."

"Well, take in from me," said Carlos. "The world is round, the earth is round. It's like a large ball. It's not like a slice of bread!"

Billy had been listening to this back-and-forth conversation. He readily agreed with Carlos and wandered why Pedro, or any other person, would believe that the world was flat.

Just then a bell rang. It was time for the afternoon meal. The three, Pedro, Carlos, and Billy went to the cook's quarters and received a plate of food topped by slices of very hard rye-flour bread.

"It's not much that we're eating," said Carlos. "I often think of the good meals that I had at home. There, my wife prepared what I wanted to eat. Here, I get whatever is thrown at me. There's a big, big difference, I'll tell you!"

"What did I tell you?" emphasized Pedro. "The crew is getting restless, not only about how far we continue to be away from home, but these lousy meals. Everyone is sick and tired of this kind of treatment. We're ready to turn back, and the sooner the better. Carlos, you sound like you're coming over to our side."

"No, not really," replied Carlos. "I still won't believe like those superstitious people—that the world is flat. We're not gonna fall off the edge of the earth. That's nonsense! Sure, the meals are bad but that's true for any long voyage. It can't be helped; it's normal to such adventures."

Two days later, in the afternoon, as he finished his meal, Billy saw the Captain, Christopher Columbus, stride by, going directly to the observation area. The Captain wanted to sight land, to reach land. Every nerve in his body was calling out for an end to this voyage—he needed to step on the shore of the Indies!

The evening was coming on, slowly getting dark. The Captain stood on the observation deck. Frequently he looked up to the crows-nest to make sure the man up there was awake and watching for any sight of land.

The date was October 11, 1492. It had been ten long weeks since they left their home port in Spain. He had tried to assure his crew members that they'd find land at any moment, but they had ceased believing him. They were now ready to mutiny.

Just as he began his watch in early evening, a sandpiper flew near the ship. Columbus's heart leapt in his breast. Surely we are close to land, he told himself. A shout came from the sister ship, the *Nina*.

"Captain," said the skipper, as he maneuvered the *Nina* closer to the *Santa Maria*, "we picked a cane and a short pole out of the water. The pole has some carvings on it. And, we retrieved a small branch with berries clinging to it. We must be near land!"

"Thank you, Captain," shouted Columbus. "Your evidence is very good, overwhelming, in fact. Keep a good lookout for I'm sure we're about to reach land."

The two ships sailed along, about a hundred feet between them. As Columbus stood stolidly, watching for any additional sign, he thought back on his difficulties in obtaining funding for his adventure and belief in his cause.

He knew he was right, that he could sail West and reach the Indies, but so many people disputed him. And, many of those were in high places. Now, with these new signs of land, he was certain that he would return to Spain in triumph.

He stared out into the darkness. Just after midnight a shout went up from the man in the crow's-nest, "A light, a light," shouted the man, high above Columbus, in the main mast in the center of the ship.

Columbus strained his eyes towards the western horizon. He thought that he saw a light moving, but it may have been his imagination. The power of suggestion was overtaking him and he was ready to believe almost anything.

Columbus & his crew look for land

Then it happened! Yes, there was a light. It was moving slowly, back and forth. It must have been a lighted torch, held high by someone. A person, a man, an inhabitant, a human being—someone is there, someone to greet them!

"Bos'n," shouted Columbus.

"Yes sir," replied the Bos'n as he hurried to the observation deck. "I hear you, sir."

"You and the First Mate must be ready," he said. "Get the First Mate here."

The First Mate came rushing from another part of the ship, ready for the Captain's instructions.

Columbus directed the Bos'n and First Mate to bring in the sails, to slow the ship. He cautioned him not to run onto a reef and further, to get ready for daylight landfall.

Billy heard the Captain calling to the Bos'n. Other sailors ran to the area as the Bos'n and First Mate gave out orders to the other sailors. They slowed the forward progress of the ship and began preparations for a landing at daylight.

Columbus slept no more that night and as dawn broke, he found himself staring at an island. Land! He had reached land! And, he had not sailed off the edge of the earth!

As objects became more visible in the early light of morning, Columbus chose a landing site. Then he gathered a team of seven men and instructed them on the procedure during landing.

"Now, men" he said, "we don't know what those people will do. We don't know if there are two or three or a hundred of them. We don't know if they are armed and intend to harm us or if they are peaceful."

"Our mission," he added, calmly but full of excitement within, "is to arrive in peace, but we must be on the alert for any danger. I will go first. My foot will be the first one that steps on the land."

"This is a momentous occasion," he continued. "We are here through the grace of God and of our sovereigns, King Ferdinand and Queen Isabella. If these be heathens, our Holy Catholic Church will help restore them to the religious community of our Savior."

"When we land," he added, "we must quickly kneel and give thanks to our Lord for safely bringing us to the Indies. We must pay tribute to His guidance over these long weeks."

As more light appeared, Columbus saw that they had come close to a small island.

"We will name that island San Salvador," said Columbus, to all within earshot. "It is our salvation and we are grateful."

The landing party was assembled and Columbus, in the first boat, was rowed to a sandy beach. He stepped out on the new land, the Indies.

About fifty yards away, less than ten natives watched him step on the beach and then kneel in thankful prayer. They watched the other sailors step on the shore and kneel to pray. It seemed like a strange ritual to them.

Billy stayed on the *Santa Maria* and watched these events. He preferred to stay on the ship because he could see all of the actions more readily.

"Well, Pedro," said Billy, "what is your opinion now? Do you want to continue your belief that the ship will fall off the edge of the earth? Also, we've reached the Indies by sailing West, not East. How about that?"

"Yes, you're right," answered Pedro, somewhat shaken, "I'm convinced that we haven't fallen off the edge of the earth just yet. But there is still more time, more territory that we don't know anything about. It could still happen."

"And, do you still think the earth is flat?" asked Billy, in a slightly teasing way.

"That, too," responded Pedro. "We have reached the Indies, just as Columbus said. But are we sure this land is the Indies? Maybe it's somewhere else. Maybe we've reached *terra incognito*—the unknown territory. It's gonna take a while before we know who these natives really are."

"Yes, you're right," said Billy. "But finding this land must have changed your thinking at least a little, hasn't it?"

"Oh, yes," replied Pedro. "I'm very open-minded. Show me the facts and I'll believe. But, remember, before we reached this land, just a few days ago, we didn't know where we were and what was about to happen. We could have been sailing open seas for years and years! Now, everything has changed, so I'm ready to face the new facts."

"That's very reasonable of you," said Billy, diplomatically. "You're on the right track. When you have the facts, then you can make a correct decision."

Suddenly, the *Santa Maria* lurched to one side, and Billy began to fall overboard. But one of the sailors grabbed Billy's sleeve and began to hang on. Billy didn't fall off the edge of the ship and as he turned to thank the sailor, he saw his wife, Thalia, smiling at him and holding on to his sleeve to keep him from falling off the couch.

"Wow! What an experience!" exclaimed Billy, as he quickly recovered his senses and realized he was in the office of Dr. Dulcamara.

"I was there! I was there when Columbus landed on San Salvador!" Billy shouted this as he was regaining consciousness here at his familiar place.

"It was great," he added. "I watched Columbus step on land, an island that he called San Salvador. I could see the natives watching Columbus and his men. As soon as they reached land, they knelt in prayer in thanks for a safe journey."

"There was a near mutiny," he went on. "Just before land was seen, the sailors were talking about turning around and going back to Spain, whether Columbus approved or not. It was a dicey time."

"But," said Thalia, as Billy slowed down, "he did get here, or there, to be exact. Somewhere in the Caribbean, no one is sure of the exact first place that they landed."

"Yes," added Billy, "discovery was made."

"And," said Thalia, "don't forget, Columbus was proved to be right. He had found land by sailing West instead of East, and, to boot, he had not sailed off the edge of the Earth," this latter said with a laugh.

"It must have been a happy time for him," continued Thalia, "because, as you point out, his crew was about ready to mutiny. They feared that they were getting too far from their homeland, Spain, and they thought that they were in some unknown land."

"That's exactly what one of the sailors said to me," replied Billy. "He called it *terra incognito*, the unknown land. Of course, Columbus's maps showed nothing in the area where he found land. That space on the map was blank."

"He was lucky," said Billy, "that he found land when he did; otherwise, I'm sure he would have turned back within a few days, and left the discovery to some later explorer."

"Well," responded Thalia, "you win some and you lose some and it appears that Columbus won this round."

"He sure did," replied Billy, looking for some commendation for his adventure. "And, I was glad to be in on this famous discovery!"

Chapter 13

Beethoven's Ninth Symphony

"I know it's about time for Thalia to undergo a trip into the past," said Billy, laughing. "She has volunteered to be the patient for this next medical session. We should have arranged for her to be in some other events, but somehow I always got the chance."

"Well," replied Dr. Dulcamara, watching Thalia hang up her coat, "that's how it goes sometimes. I'm sure that Thalia will enjoy the trip back into history, just as you have."

"I've been dying to go," said Thalia, enthusiastically. "Billy keeps being the main patient, but he has allowed me to go on this trip, this time."

"So, have you decided on who you want to see in this session?" asked the doctor.

"Yes, I have," announced Thalia, with assurance. "I will be trying to visit one of my favorite composers, Ludwig von Beethoven! He died not too long ago, in 1827 but his music lives on."

"I love his music," said the doctor. "It is stirring and he was such a master at conveying his feelings. His *Pastoral Symphony*, number six, I believe, is so delightful. I can just feel like I'm walking with him in the countryside."

"I love that symphony, too," beamed Thalia. "But, my true favorite is his *Ninth Symphony*. That's the greatest music I've ever heard!"

"Well, let's get you off to see Beethoven, we hope," said the doctor.

"Yes," answered Thalia. "I know that we can't be sure of where we'll find ourselves, but I'm hoping to be in Vienna when Beethoven is there."

"You know the routine," said Dr. Dulcamara, as he began preparations for the hypnotic session. "You've watched Billy do it a number of times."

"Yes," responded Thalia, as she took a seat on the couch and arranged some of the pillows behind her.

Billy pulled up a chair just behind Thalia, ready to help in any way that might be necessary.

"What I want you to do," said the doctor, "is look intently at this drawing of a treble chord. Keep staring at it. I will hum a tune and you will keep staring. Try not to blink."

Thalia stared at the image of the treble chord as the doctor began to hum a passage from one of Beethoven's works. In a few seconds her eyes closed and she, with Billy's help, slowly sank back on the pillows.

"It's time to get up, miss," said the hotel maid. "You've been sleeping in a little later than you intended."

"Oh, my," replied Thalia, "what time is it?"

"A little past seven," answered the maid. "The manager told me to come up and waken you. He said you wanted to get up at six and when you did not appear, he sent me up to tell you that it's time to get up."

"Thank you, thank you," replied Thalia, as she quickly washed her face and combed her hair. She donned her clothes and went downstairs for breakfast.

After breakfast, she walked around the streets of Vienna, stopping for lunch in a restaurant. It was Springtime, the parks were full of newly-emerging flowers and most of the trees had their new leaves. The sunshine was warm but not hot, it was only the first week of May.

In mid-afternoon, Thalia walked to a plaza in front of St. Stephen's Church. She sat on a bench breathing in the airs of Spring. Nearby a trio of musicians played—there was a violin, a viola, and a cello. They played music of Mozart, Schubert, and Beethoven. Not far away was a solo violinist playing music of Mozart. It was a magical time for Thalia.

As she listened to the music and as the afternoon wore on, a couple came and sat on the same bench. They nodded "Guten Tag" to Thalia. She smiled and nodded in response, grateful to the couple for noticing her.

"Is Herr Beethoven's new symphony going to be played tonight?" asked the lady of her escort.

"It might be," he replied. "As I understand it, Beethoven wanted the premier of this symphony to take place in Berlin, but I think his friends have talked him out of taking it out of town. They want the first playing to happen here."

"Why did he want it premiered in Berlin?" asked the lady. "He's lived here for many years. It should be first played in his home city."

"Well," responded the man, "as you know, Herr Beethoven is pretty stubborn. He needs to get his way. He feels like Vienna has given over its taste in music to the Italians; that German composers, like him, have had to take a back seat to the musicians from the south, from Italy."

"Of course," he added, "we do have that wonderful Italian composer, Giocchino Rossini. He's all the rage now. But I hear that he wants to move away from us here in Vienna; he intends to go to Paris"

"Yes," replied the lady, "Well, the Italians do make tuneful and lovely music. But Beethoven is special. Sure, he can be cantankerous. There was that time when he was going to dedicate his Third Symphony, the *Eroica*, to Napoleon Bonaparte. But, when Napoleon declared himself Emperor, he changed the dedication."

146

"And, change it he did," emphasized the man. "He dedicated it to 'a great man', or something like that. As I understand, he tore off the part of the front page where he had written Napoleon's name. When he makes up his mind on something, no one can change it and he knows it."

"Now that he is deaf," added the man, "it must be a terrible trial for him, to write music that he can barely hear. He can't hear all the nuances of the sounds—and that's so important to any composer."

"I don't know how he does it," responded the lady. "Didn't he contemplate suicide once?"

"Yes, yes, some years, ago," he replied. "When he was residing at Heiligenstadt, he wrote a letter or a statement about his deafness. I've read it; it was very moving. Like you, I can't understand how he can continue to compose such lovely music while he is deaf! It's beyond me."

"Well, we'd best get going," said the lady. "We want to attend the concert tonight."

"Right you are," replied the man. "Where is it to be performed?"

"At the Karntnertortheater," said the lady. "We have time to eat and then go to the concert."

The couple got up from the park bench and walked away from the park. Thalia sat for a few moments. She, too, intended to attend the concert. She decided to get something to eat, and then go to the theater.

After her meal, Thalia walked to the theater, bought her ticket, and went inside to take her seat. She sat next to a young college student. They chatted.

"Hello, my name is Helga," said the student. "The playbill says that Herr Beethoven's Ninth Symphony is to be played for the first time."

"It's nice to meet you," replied Thalia. "My name is Thalia and, yes, the Ninth Symphony is supposed to be premiered this evening. I certainly hope so."

Thalia looked around, the hall was filling quickly; soon every seat was taken and some people stood against the walls at the back.

Beethoven leads the orchestra in his Ninth Symphony

The music began with an overture, *Die Weihe des Hauses*. After that came parts of the *Missa Solemnis*. There was an intermission and the audience again took their seats.

Beethoven came onto the stage to direct the performance of his Ninth Symphony. He was wildly applauded. Cheers rang out for this fifty-four year-old well-loved composer. He bowed to the audience. He took his place at the front of the orchestra, a music stand in front of him that held the music, although he knew all the notes by heart.

Moments later, a second conductor appeared from the left side of the stage. He received modest applause. Actually he was to be the **real** conductor. Beethoven, being deaf, could not hear most of the notes that were being played.

The other conductor, Michael Umlauf, had instructed the musicians and singers to ignore Beethoven's directions and to focus on him, Umlauf. And, it was a good thing that the musicians followed Umlauf. Beethoven frequently was several notes, even measures, ahead or behind—he just could NOT hear. Beethoven, at this performance, was giving directions to a group of musicians who were (without him knowing it) ignoring him! They were following the direction of conductor Umlauf.

The symphony lasted about ninety minutes. As the last note rang out, Beethoven, who was a few notes behind, was still conducting and directing. But, he soon stopped.

The audience was on its feet. The jubilant applause nearly brought on an earthquake. Nothing like this symphony had ever been heard before. And, Vienna had the premier.

As the audience continued to applaud, the soprano, Caroline Unger, tears in her eyes, walked over to Beethoven. She gently turned him around to face the audience.

"See, Maestro," she said, aware that he couldn't hear her words, "they are applauding you!"

Beethoven looked out to the crowd. Everyone was standing and applauding. Many waved hats while others took handkerchiefs and other cloths from their pockets and waved them—they realized that Beethoven could see them applaud but he couldn't hear them! However, he could see the cloths being waved at him and recognize their enthusiasm.

"This is wonderful, Helga," said Thalia to her new friend. "Oh, this is wonderful. I'm so happy even though my eyes are wet with tears."

"Mine, too," laughed Helga, as she dabbed at her eyes. "To be here and see this, actually to feel this, is a highlight of my life. I'm laughing for joy although I feel for that great man and his inability to hear his own music."

"Yes, it's tragic," said Thalia, compassionately. "He can't even hear the applause that is being generously given to him. He certainly deserves every accolade that can be bestowed on him."

"I've just counted that they've brought him back onto the stage five times!" exclaimed Helga. "In Vienna, it's customary for royalty to have three ovations, so our hero, Herr Beethoven, has outdone the Royal Court! What a national hero!"

"That's amazing," said Thalia, "especially when you remember that Beethoven is not a part of the Royal Court, and is just a musician. Musicians are often considered as very low servants at the Royal Court."

"Has this ever happened before?" asked Thalia.

Helga had disappeared and a man answered: "Yes, this probably has happened sometime, I suppose."

It was Billy, her husband. He was helping her to keep her balance as she sat on Dr. Dulcamara's sofa. She had nearly tumbled off as she clapped her hands, applauding Beethoven and his Ninth Symphony.

"You were clapping your hands," said Billy. "Why?"

"Oh," answered Thalia, as she more fully recovered from her trip to dreamland. "I was clapping for Beethoven. I was part of the audience and we applauded him. We had just heard the first performance of Beethoven's Ninth Symphony in Vienna."

"So, you got to Vienna," said Billy, happily. "And, you got to hear the premier of Beethoven's Ninth Symphony. What a treat for you!"

"Oh, dear," responded Thalia, full of glee and happiness, "it was a treat, you can say that again! I was there. I saw the great man, Beethoven, himself!"

"Oh, doctor," she said, as she reached out to touch his arm, "Thank you, thank you, for that wonderful experience. For me, to see Beethoven as a living person was wonderful! I'm just so full of happiness!"

"Well," replied Dr. Dulcamara, "you're certainly welcome. But, you provided the event. All I did was to hypnotize you and put you into a dreamlike state. You had already predisposed your mind to being in Vienna to attend the concert of Beethoven's music. You must take some of the credit, maybe most of it."

Thalia rattled on for another five or ten minutes, telling the doctor and Billy about her wonderful adventure.

That evening, after dinner, she sat at her piano and played music for about an hour. It was all Beethoven's music. Billy, proud of his wife's ability, eagerly listened. He was happy on two accounts: for the lovely music of the master, Beethoven, and for the skill of his darling wife, Thalia, who played the music like a virtuoso.

She was happy, he was happy—all brought about by a long-dead composer, Ludwig von Beethoven.

Chapter 14

George Washington Dies

"Dr. Dulcamara," said Billy, "I've done a lot of traveling through your efforts at experimental hypnosis. These sessions have allowed me to go back in history, to be present at events that I learned about when I was a student in elementary school."

"Well," replied the doctor, "we've both profited. You have experienced history and I've been able to study you while you were under the hypnotic spell. So, it's been good for you and good for me."

"Don't forget me," said Billy's wife, Thalia. "I, too, had a wonderful trip back to Egypt, to one of my heroines, the great queen, Cleopatra. And, I saw Beethoven in Vienna."

"Well, it seems like this whole experimental time has been rewarding to everyone concerned," said the doctor, smiling and bowing towards Thalia.

'I'd like to do a few more sessions," he added. "Can you spare me the time for one or two more?"

"Yes, I can," replied Billy, enthusiastically. "This has turned into a wonderful experience for me and I'm willing to go on, if you're willing to continue."

"In that case," said the doctor, "let's get ready for a new session."

"I'm ready to go!" said Billy, as he took a seat on the sofa and he and Thalia arranged some pillows behind him.

"And, where are you going this time?" asked the doctor.

"To George Washington," replied Billy. "He was the greatest president and leader of our country. He died in 1799, barely fifty years ago. I want to be there at his death."

"Fine," said Dr. Dulcamara. "Let me get my notebook and I'll be ready in just a few minutes. It won't take long and you'll be back in 1799."

Thalia brought up a chair to be closer to Billy and the doctor gathered a notebook, a thermometer, and other instruments that he would use to make measurements while Billy was in dreamland.

"All right," said the doctor. "Now, Billy, I want you to look closely at this pencil as I hold it before you. I'll move it a little up or down but you must stare intently at it."

"I will do what you ask," said Billy, as he stared fixedly at the pencil the doctor was holding slightly above his head. He kept staring at it and suddenly he eased back on the pillows; he was in dreamland.

"Is that my husband out there in the rain?" asked Martha Washington.

"Yes, ma'am," answered the overseer who was standing on the large front porch of the mansion at Mount Vernon. "He's been measuring the changes he wants to make on the front lawn."

The front lawn of the mansion was level out for about fifty feet, and then it slowly sloped downward towards the Potomac River. It was a beautiful expanse and lent an air of quietude and pleasantness to the magnificent view from the porch.

It was Friday the 13th of December in the year 1799. Martha's husband, George, the General who had led the patriot army that had beaten the British and won independence for the thirteen colonies, now called the United States of America, and who had been the first president of the country, had been home for a little over two years.

George Washington could have been president until he died, but he refused a third four-year term. He wanted to return to his home, to his Mount Vernon estate and be with his sweetheart, his wife, Martha.

King George, the Third, of Britain, when told that Washington was going to leave public service and return home, could not believe it. He knew that any man who had tasted power like Washington had, that it would be impossible to give up that power. King George said: "If he relinquishes power, he will be the greatest man in the world!"

But Washington did relinquish that power. Unlike most men, he did not let the power corrupt him. He had served his country well and, when his second four-year presidential term was done, he wanted to go home.

"It's time for others to come forward and take the reins of the country," he was quoted as saying. "I've earned my rest and I want to go home and spend my last years there."

George Washington was not given to long speeches. His first inaugural address was only 133 words long and it took only ninety seconds for him to deliver it.

But, this day, in mid-December, was raw and cold. While he was out on the large lawn, preparing for its renovation, the cold rain turned to sleet. He was wet throughout when he came back into the house. The previous day, the 12th, he'd been caught outside during a snowstorm, and had been wet to his skin.

Martha called to him, to come in for a warm drink. She wanted him to get out of the weather, especially since he had a raw throat from the previous day.

George followed his wife's wishes and, handing his horse off to a servant, trudged into the house. Before he entered, he shook off his outer garments, scattering frozen raindrops and some snowflakes onto the porch.

"Here's your change, dear," said Martha, as he laid out dry, warm clothes for him.

"Thank you, my dear," replied George. "I'll just towel off and put on the new ones you've laid out for me. I'd also like that warm drink that you spoke of, maybe a cup of tea or a dram of brandy."

"Well, my dear sir," responded Martha, happy to have him inside where it was warm, "you'll get both. When you've changed, come into the sitting room and they'll be ready there for you. I'll go now to see that they get done."

"Thank you, my dear," said George.

He changed into dry clothes and then went into the sitting room to be with Martha while he had the tea and the brandy. She, too, had a cup of hot tea.

Several servants, including Billy, stood against the walls of the room, ready to respond to any request by either Martha or George.

A few minutes after drinking, he said to Martha: "Those were nice hot drinks, but somehow I still feel chilly, and my throat hurts. I guess I got over-chilled when I was outside."

"Yes, I'm sure of that," replied his wife. "And, you remember yesterday, you were not feeling well when you came inside. You must remember that you're not as young as you once were. You're not far from seventy and you must keep that in mind."

"Oh, I'm still strong," said George, with a laugh. "We men never think we're old. That's only for those old people who need canes when they walk. I need no cane. I can get along quite well."

"Yes, dear," said Martha, resignedly. "Would you like some more tea or brandy or both?"

"No," replied George. "I've had enough, thank you."

"Well," said Martha, "we'll begin supper before long. That should warm you up better than those drinks. Please stay inside and let the cold rain stay outside. It's better for you that you not get wet and cold any more."

"You're right, my dear," he replied. "I do have a sore throat and it seems to be getting worse."

George went into his study. In an hour or so, a servant came in to tell him that supper was ready.

George went to the dining room. There, on the table, was a heaping dish of mashed potatoes with coconut, his favorite. Also, another large dish of pineapple slices, another favorite. But he shivered as he sat down at the table. He was cold inside. He really had not felt warm since he came in out of the cold rain.

"I'm sorry, my dear," he said to Martha, "somehow I'm not hungry. My sore throat won't let me swallow; it hurts too much. I will have some more hot tea, though."

Martha quickly poured him some tea and he sipped it, as the others laid into the delicious food.

After supper, he said to Martha: "I need to write out some plans and designs, so I'll be in my study."

"All right, my dear," she replied. "Don't overwork yourself. Remember you can do more tomorrow. Perhaps you should rest yourself today. There's no big rush to get things done just now. Whatever you have to do surely can wait until tomorrow or for a few days."

"My dear," admonished her husband, "you've known me all these years and you know that I never put off until tomorrow what I can do today. It just wouldn't make me feel right. I'm a stickler for that, I know, but I'm so used to that discipline that I can't help myself. There are things to do, and I must do them."

Martha retired to her sitting room and, after several hours, she went to their bedroom. She expected George to soon mount the stairs and join her. At times, she dozed off, but she couldn't maintain her sleep, not while her husband toiled away in another room.

Soon, she heard the stair squeak, indicating he was on the way to her. George entered the bedroom.

"I really don't feel very well," he said.

"And, you don't look it, either," replied Martha, as she turned to look more closely at him. "I'll ask one of the servants to go to bring the doctor."

"No," said George, hoarsely, "let me sleep it off; I'm sure that I'll feel better in the morning."

But later on, about 3:00am, he woke Martha. He could barely speak, his throat was so sore.

"I'll send Caroline, my girl, to get the doctor," said Martha.

"No," replied George. "I don't want you to get up. You'll get cold and you will be sick with something. Caroline will come in to light the fire soon and then you can tell her to go for the doctor."

About two hours later, Caroline came in to light the fire, and Martha spoke to her. Albin Rawlins, the overseer, came in at the same time. He had watched the General earlier in the day and suspected that he might be sick.

"Mr. Rawlins, send someone for Dr. Craik. Get him here as soon as possible," Martha told the overseer. "And, notify Dr. Dick and Dr. Brown to come as soon as possible."

Messengers dashed away to those people. Dr. James Craik, the General's friend and personal physician, lived nearby, and he arrived before nine a.m.

Dr. Elisha Dick arrived at 3:00pm and Dr. Gustavus Brown arrived shortly after that. Soon all three doctors were at the bedside of the obviously very sick George Washington.

Billy and several other servants stood against the wall, ready to follow any instruction.

"What is he doing now?" whispered Billy to another servant.

"He's taking some blood," answered the other. "It's called blood-letting and it's supposed to take the bad stuff, the evil cause of the sickness, out of the body with the blood."

Meanwhile, George lay on his bed, suffering quietly. Mr. Rawlins, the overseer, had bled the General before Dr. Craik arrived. Bleeding was a common practice often done by a non-medical, trusted servant.

"What's he doing now?" again asked Billy of his friend.

"That's a poultice," answered the other man. "It's made of various ground-up stuff and is put on the chest or the throat to help with the cure. Sometimes they use mustard and that feels awful warm, even hot. It helps to pull out the bad stuff that's causing the sickness."

Dr Craik applied the poultice to George's throat, laying it fully around the front. The warmth felt good. The doctor bled the General again.

By mid-afternoon, the General was no better and it was very difficult for him to talk, it hurt so much. Also, he could barely swallow. Dr. Craik gave him a mixture to gargle or swallow, but he could do neither, nearly choking in the process.

The doctors often examined the General and then moved to a far corner of the room to discuss their findings.

"Dr. Craik," asked Dr. Brown, "what is your diagnosis?"

"He has a throat problem, maybe a lung problem," said Dr. Craik. "It's a breathing problem, but it's more centrally located in his throat. It's best to bleed him at this time," he added, as Dr. Dick nodded his agreement.

"So, we're agreed that bleeding will be the best remedy?" asked Dr. Brown. "Are there other remedies that we should try first?"

"No," said Dr. Dick, quietly but professionally. "My experience tells me that bleeding is the prime remedy right now for the patient."

"All right," said Dr. Brown. "Dr. Dick, the patient has already been bled twice. Is it wise to bleed him further?"

"It's the recommended procedure," reply Dr. Dick. "We should follow what has worked before to cure others."

"You're right," answered Dr. Brown. "Dr. Dick, would you please perform the procedure? Meanwhile, Dr. Craik and I will see to making him as comfortable as possible."

Dr. Dick proceeded and the other two doctors asked that warm blankets be brought to the bed. They wrapped the warm blankets around George.

"My feet are so cold," said George. Quickly Dr. Brown asked one of the servants to remove his socks and massage his feet. Another servant brought a warming pan and it was placed against the soles of his feet and a blanket tucked in so the warming pan would stay.

"Are you feeling any better, sir?" asked Dr. Craik of the General.

"No," answered George. "I still feel cold in my chest area and I'm chilly very much throughout my whole body."

At one point, Martha Washington, who had left the room, came back and talked to the doctors about the excessive blood-letting. She did not believe that copious bleeding was helpful; she asked the doctors to not do any more blood-letting.

The three doctors conferred again and again. Their remedies did not seem to help the patient. He was steadily getting worse and he could not talk to them without a great deal of pain in his throat.

George Washington dies.

Mr. Tobias Lear, who had been the General's personal secretary, was present during all of this time. He stood quietly in the room, ready to supply any help that was asked of him.

"Mr. Lear, please bring Martha here," said George, hoarsely and almost in a whisper. "I want to talk to her. Do it quickly."

George didn't realize that his wife, Martha, was sitting near his bed. She had earlier left the room but had recently returned. She heard him speak to Tobias Lear.

Martha stood up at once and Mr. Lear told her that her husband wanted to talk to her. She bent over to hear what he had to say.

"Dear," said George, barely whispering, "in my study, the middle drawer of my desk, there are two papers. They are two Wills. Please go with Tobias and bring them to me."

Martha, accompanied by Tobias, went to George's study. She found the two papers, the two Wills, and took them to her husband.

"This one," said George, again struggling against the pain of speaking, "is to be discarded and destroyed; it is an earlier Will. This other one is my final Will. I think that shortly you will need it."

With that statement it appeared that George Washington was preparing himself to die. He seemed to know that the end was near and that whatever the doctors were doing was not being sufficiently effective.

"I'm not afraid to die," whispered George, to Dr. Craik, who leaned over him. "I'm ready."

"We don't want you to go," replied Dr. Craik. "We're doing the proper treatments to keep you here with us. Please do not leave us."

"When a man's time comes," said George, "he should not stay, but he should go. This, I think, is my time. It has come for me and I must go as required."

Dr. Craik again conferred with the other two doctors.

"He appears to be ready to die," said Dr. Craik. "He seems to be at peace with himself. Our treatments, our remedies, do not seem to be helping him. Have either of you any further suggestions as to what we should do?"

"I'm sorry to say that I have no further ideas," said Dr. Brown.

"Nor I," responded Dr. Dick.

"Colonel Lear," said Dr. Brown to the Colonel, a long-time friend of Washington, "have you any suggestion to make?"

"No, sir, I do not," replied the colonel, quickly and quietly. "My knowledge of medicine is slight and this seems to be a medical problem. I sorely wish I could help my dear friend but I have no medical help in me." He was almost in tears as he said that.

The three doctors, Colonel Lear, Martha, the overseers, and the other onlookers were at a loss as to what to do. The great man, George Washington, lay in the bed, seemingly ready to die, to greet his maker.

Slowly, but deliberately, George Washington folded his hands on his chest. He opened his eyes to look lovingly at his darling wife, Martha. She began to weep quietly. He closed his eyes and gave a deep sigh. His chest heaved and fell silent. George Washington had passed on to another world.

Billy, along with the other servants standing against the wall of the bedroom, had heard and seen all. He was in tears. Everyone in the room was crying.

Dr. Brown felt the patient's pulse.

"There is no pulse," he said, quietly.

Martha, trying not to, found herself sobbing.

"Is he gone?" she asked.

Dr. Brown shook his head in the affirmative.

"I'm glad it's over," she said quietly, "I'll soon follow him. There are not any more trials for me to go through."

Caroline, her maid, took her arm and together, they slowly walked from the room.

"A truly great man has just left us," said Dr. Brown. "We will not see his likes again in our lifetime."

"Amen to that," responded Dr. Craik. "He was larger than any man in our country. It's too bad that Fate has cut him down now, just when he so much enjoyed his retirement, his Mount Vernon, his home, his family."

"I'll never see anyone as great as he," said Dr. Dick. "It's been my privilege to be his friend."

"And, my privilege, too," said Colonel Lear. "We were close and I will always remember our times together."

Some of the servants, including Billy, slowly left the room. They went down the stairs. Billy walked out onto the large porch area and looked over the green, grassy lawn, towards the Potomac River.

He turned to see a young lady. It was nighttime, and the face that he was looking at was barely visible. Suddenly she said: "Sweetheart, it's time for you to wake up. You've been in dreamland for nearly an hour!"

"Oh," said Billy, as he recognized his wife. "I am a bit confused. I was at George Washington's house. It's called Mount Vernon. And, he died there. It was so sad."

"So, you did get to visit George Washington?" asked Thalia. "But it was at a sad time for you, wasn't it?"

"Yes," said Billy, sitting up and still trying to come back to full consciousness. "That was a difficult time. Our hero, the Father of our Country, died. I stood there and watched the whole thing. I still can't get over it. I'll just need more time to cope with it. I really feel bad."

Meanwhile, Dr. Dulcamara was rapidly writing notes as Billy talked to Thalia. This session had gone very well and he was happy with his experiment in putting Billy under hypnosis.

"You have tears in your eyes!" exclaimed Thalia.

"I suppose so," answered Billy, soberly. "It was truly a very, very sad time. I've never seen anyone die before and I watched that for several hours, it seems. I'm so sad."

"But, my dear," replied Thalia. "It happened a long time ago, in 1799. This is the middle of the 1850's, fifty years later."

"Yes, I know," said Billy, "but it seemed like I was back there in December of 1799—just a few minutes ago. It was so very real."

"Billy," said Dr. Dulcamara, "I think these experiments are becoming too real. We need to take a break of a month or two where we don't do these."

"You've been a wonderful patient," he added. "But you need a rest. And, maybe I need a rest. I need to take some time to review my notes and try to determine what I've learned from our experiments. I may attend a conference."

"That's a good idea," said Billy. "And, next time we do some we need to involve my wife, Thalia, more. She needs to be the main patient."

"Yes," agreed Thalia, "I'd like that. Lead me on!"

Chapter 15

Finale

"My good friend," said Billy to Dr. Dulcamara, "we want you to come to supper at our house next Thursday evening. Can you make yourself available?"

"Oh, yes," responded the doctor, happily. "Your wife is such a good cook that I would drop almost everything to have a meal at your home."

"Then it's settled," said Billy. "We'll look for you anytime after 5:00pm."

"I'll be there," replied the doctor. "And, thank you kindly for the invitation."

On Thursday evening, Dr. Dulcamara arrived at the Costello residence carrying a fine appetite and a bottle of wine. He was greeted by Billy, who accepted the gift, and set it on the table—it was to be part of the meal.

Thalia came from the kitchen and greeted Dr. Dulcamara, then returned to continue preparing the meal.

Soon after, Thalia called: "Billy, help me here a little now that you've got the doctor settled. I need you."

"Yes, my dear," replied Billy, as he went into the kitchen to help his wife. In a few minutes, he returned to be with the doctor.

"My wife is preparing my favorite meal," said Billy, "and I'm only too glad to help. We're going to eat roast pork and sauerkraut with mashed potatoes."

"That's a truly wonderful meal," said the doctor, sniffing the pleasant aromas from the kitchen.

"This is a favorite meal that I often cook for my favorite hero," said Thalia, as she poked her head out of the kitchen to advise the doctor of what was happening.

"Yes," added Billy, laughing, as he arose to acknowledge her presence, "this is a meal prepared and shared with my favorite heroine."

Soon all was ready and they sat at their places around the table. The two men dug into the food with second and third helpings. Very little was said as they enjoyed the wonderful cooking of Thalia. They dined well that evening and Thalia received compliments from the two men.

At one point, Dr. Dulcamara leaned back in his chair, smiled at Thalia, and said: "Without doubt, this is the finest food I've eaten in California—that is, since the last time I had a meal at your house!"

This brought a happy laugh from Thalia. She said: "Thank You, doctor. It's just basic, ordinary food, cooked with loving care."

"That must be the secret ingredient—loving care," exclaimed the doctor. "You have the magic touch and you put in that extra ingredient—loving care!"

"She sure does," interjected Billy. "Thalia not only knows what to cook and how to do it, she also enjoys making delicious dishes for others, especially me!" he laughed.

As they finished the main course, Thalia brought out a serving of blueberry pie.

"Blueberry pie!" exclaimed a happy Dr. Dulcamara. "What a treat! What a treat! My goodness, I feel like I've died and gone to heaven!" he laughed as he dug into the pie.

After dessert, Thalia said: "It's warm in here. Let's go outside and sit on the front porch."

"Great idea," exclaimed Billy, and they carried their glasses of wine there.

Outside, they began to discuss the hypnotic sessions that they'd had with Dr. Dulcamara as part of his medical experiments.

"Do you feel that your experiments were worthwhile and helpful to your research?" asked Billy.

"Without a doubt!" exclaimed the doctor. "What we were able to accomplish was unique. To my knowledge, no other doctor has done such experiments, at least to the extensive degree that I've done them. I now know a great deal more about treating my patients with hypnotism, thanks to you both."

"Well," said Thalia, "we've gained, too. We've been able to participate in historical events that we knew only from books and stories. We have learned a lot."

"Let us review, my dear," said Billy to his wife, "what all that we've learned from our journeys into the past. Let us count some of the ways."

"Well," replied Thalia, "first off, we were able to be present at great moments in history. And, with people who made a special historical mark. That's something very few people, perhaps nobody else, has done."

"Yes," answered Billy, "thanks to Dr. Dulcamara. If he hadn't wanted to do that hypnosis research, where would we have been? And, although we were only actually dreaming about an event, when we woke up we had the real-life feeling of just having been there and done that!"

"Until we began working with Dr. Dulcamara," he added, "we knew these heroic people only from our lessons in school."

"And," said Thalia, "that's what every student gets— the story of a hero or heroine from the schoolbooks. And, basically, that's it. But we experienced much more."

"Yes," added Billy, "when Dr. Dulcamara put us under the hypnotic spell, it allowed us to participate in the real event, with the real persons. That was fabulous. Dreams are something all of us have, but to dream about the very subject that one aims to dream about—that's almost miraculous!"

"And, think of the future," exclaimed Thalia. "If the good doctor decides to do more research, we might be able to visit Joan of Arc, Charlemagne, Galileo, the Pilgrim landing on Plymouth Rock, Bach and Haydn!"

"Yes, yes," added Billy, with similar enthusiasm, "and Alfred the Great, Robin Hood, Beowulf, the Alamo—oh, there are so many more!"

Dr. Dulcamara had been listening to this enthusiastic discussion by husband and wife. He sat smiling, keenly aware that he was observing an intelligent couple, a husband and wife, with a wonderfully youthful outlook. They were discussing their experiences and adventures under his direction, and expecting to add more visits to famous people of the past.

"Let me say something," said the doctor. "I so much admire you both. It's a joy for me to listen to you discussing the results of your participation in my experiments. And, with your youthful enthusiasm, you are ready to set off on new adventures. My, oh my, what a delightful couple!"

"Some people," he added, "simply follow the rules, they do what they are told to do. But you two have made an adventure out of each session. You are thoughtful people. If you ever run for office," he laughed, "and if I have voting rights, I'll vote for both of you!"

"Thank you for the compliment," said Billy, laughing. "I, too, feel so blessed that my partner, my companion, my wife, that girl sitting right there," he pointed towards Thalia, who was smiling broadly, "is the finest woman I could ever imagine for me to have as a wife. I'm so grateful that she is arm-in-arm with me."

"Thanks, darling," said Thalia, as she smiled her gracious smile.

"Well," said Dr. Dulcamara, "it's time for me to go. Thank you so very much for a fine meal and a fine evening."

"And," responded Thalia, as she and Billy rose to see the doctor to the door, "thank you for the wonderful experiences that you allowed us to have. If you decide to do more experiments along this line, please include us."

Billy nodded in the affirmative as the doctor took his leave.